MYSTERIES
= AT =
SEA

PERIL
ON THE
ATLANTIC

For my dad, who loved the sea.

First published in the UK in 2023 by Usborne Publishing Limited, Usborne House, 83-85 Saffron Hill, London EC1N 8RT, England, usborne.com.

Usborne Verlag, Usborne Publishing Limited, Prüfeninger Str. 20, 93049 Regensburg, Deutschland VK Nr. 17560

Cover, inside illustrations and map by Marco Guadalupi © Usborne Publishing Limited, 2023.

Photo of Ann-Marie Howell © Tom Soper, 2021.

A CIP catalogue record for this book is available from the British Library.

Trade paperback ISBN 9781801316743

Waterstones exclusive paperback 9781805078098

7709/1 JFMAM JASOND/23

Printed and bound using 100% renewable energy at CPI Group (UK) Ltd, Croydon, CR0 4YY.

MIX
Paper | Supporting responsible forestry
FSC® C171272

MYSTERIES =AT= SEA

PERIL ON THE ATLANTIC

A. M. HOWELL

USBORNE

CONTENTS

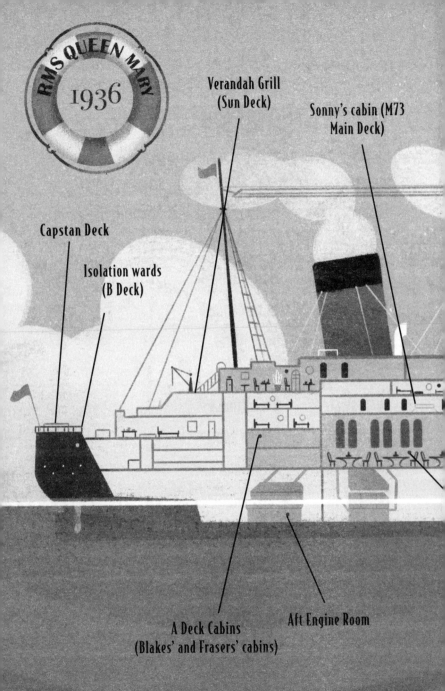

RMS QUEEN MARY
1936

Verandah Grill
(Sun Deck)

Sonny's cabin (M73
Main Deck)

Capstan Deck

Isolation wards
(B Deck)

A Deck Cabins
(Blakes' and Frasers' cabins)

Aft Engine Room

Gymnasium & Dog Kennels
(Sun Deck)

Promenade Deck
and Shops

Alice's cabin
(Sports Deck)

Wheelhouse

First Class
restaurant
(C Deck)

First Class Swimming Pool
(D Deck)

Luggage Hold/Garage

Chapter 1

QUEEN MARY

A buzz of anticipation and excitement made Alice's fingers tingle, as she stepped away from the station platform and onto the dock. Grey smoke puffed lazily from the red and black-tipped funnels of the *Queen Mary* into the hot July air, like three simmering pots preparing to boil. She sucked in a breath of awe. It was the largest vessel she had ever seen, its riveted hull so tall it blotted out the sun. Her father had said that, if the ship was placed vertically from bow to stern, it would even be taller than the Eiffel Tower in Paris!

Looking around, Alice saw that the other passengers

from the train she had travelled on to Southampton docks had already hurried off to the baggage hall, leaving her alone. She glanced at her watch. Her father had promised to meet her from the train and he was late. As she looked for him, the clamour of noise was like a discordant band as motor cars expelled expectant passengers, and giant cranes with claw-like feet sent packages cocooned in rope nets into the ship's cavernous hold.

Alice's jaw dropped in awe at the sight of a fancy black car trussed up with straps as it was swung high above her head and onto the vessel. This was a world away from the quiet Suffolk boarding school she had left that morning and she felt pleasantly giddy – to think she would soon be steaming across the Atlantic Ocean to New York!

Tightening her grip on her brown suitcase, Alice noticed it looked positively ancient in comparison to the smart leather trunks and cases being loaded onto trolleys by scurrying porters dressed in white jackets and black bow ties. A brisk nudge in the ribs caused her to stumble and loosen her grip on her suitcase. It landed on the ground with a thump. Feeling a jolt of annoyance, she bent to pick it up, but the person who had bumped into her got there first.

A harassed-looking young man in a starched cream uniform dusted down Alice's case and returned it to her.

"I'm sorry. I wasn't looking where I was going," he said anxiously. His name badge was pinned to his jacket at an odd angle, as if placed there in a hurry. *Joseph Wilks. Cabin Steward.* Alice noticed the steward's hands were trembling. He saw Alice looking and pushed them into his trouser pockets. "I hope there's nothing breakable in there," he continued.

Alice's throat pinched momentarily as she considered one very precious item inside her case. It was not breakable, but she thought the steward would not understand its importance. "No, it's fine. Please don't worry," she said.

The steward seemed distracted, his eyes darting around the dock. "I'm sorry again. I hope you enjoy your voyage, miss." He pressed on towards the crew gangway, his shoulders hunched as he wound his way round a porter's trolley stacked with five cages of twittering canaries.

Alice grinned at the sight of the birds and drew closer to get a better look. One bird was an almost luminous shade of yellow and its tiny voice strained valiantly to compete with the surrounding noise.

"Do watch out!" barked a man in a dark suit and spotless white gloves who was walking alongside the trolley. "The baroness will not tolerate any bumps or knocks to her precious birds."

Alice shrank back and watched as the cages were steered towards the first-class passenger gangway and carefully carried aboard. There was the pop and flare of a flashbulb as a ship's photographer recorded the moment. He glanced at Alice and walked over as he fiddled with his camera. "People take all sorts on board with them these days. On the last voyage a lord and lady took sixty pieces of luggage for a two-week trip to America. I could have fitted the contents of my house in their bags twice over!" Shaking his head in disbelief, he began to move through the throngs of passengers, searching out another photographic opportunity.

At the thought of mingling with baronesses, lords and ladies on the ship, Alice felt a new elation. The glamour of it all! She had longed to travel by sea her whole life, and while her aunt's accident meant this voyage had come about in an unfortunate way, she was determined to make the best of things. She stood on tiptoe and looked again for her father. He was always punctual when he came to visit her at boarding school during his snatched days of shore leave. What was keeping him?

Long queues had formed at the gangways and Alice's eyes roamed over the orchestra of waving hands and extravagantly blown kisses, as ladies in fashionable wide-legged slacks and gentlemen in rakish straw hats embarked. Licking a finger and rubbing at a spot of dirt on her skirt and tucking in her blouse, her view was suddenly obscured by a young porter pushing a trolley stacked haphazardly with luggage. His cheeks strained with exertion as his slight frame struggled to steer a path through the bustle of passengers. Alice swallowed a gasp of horror as a large suitcase wobbled precariously close to a family absorbed in a tearful farewell.

"I say...wait a moment," she called as she hurried after him, her own case bumping against her bare legs.

While the porter turned and saw Alice gesturing at the wobbling suitcase, a noisy seagull wheeled and screeched above their heads as if also alerting him to the precarious situation. The porter's eyes widened and he set about rearranging the luggage at once. Adjusting his bow tie and wiping his brow, he nodded at Alice. "Thanks for the warning, miss."

The skin at the corners of the boy's brown eyes was creased, which made Alice think he smiled a good deal, but at that moment he looked along the dock nervously. "I'm not used to pushing these trolleys. I'm a bellboy working on the ship's passenger lifts, you see. They needed extra help dockside today, but they didn't tell me I'd need the muscles of Tarzan to do the job," he said, throwing a look of regret at his spindly arms.

"Charlie! Hurry up with that luggage," yelled a puce-faced man standing further along the dock by several empty pallets.

"Oh dear. He doesn't seem happy," said Alice. The man now had his hands on his hips and was glaring at Charlie.

Charlie grimaced. "I'd best get the job finished." He set off again determinedly with the trolley, but the luggage creaked in protest and listed to the side once more.

Alice felt a twinge of concern. She really ought to wait for her father, but she did not want Charlie to get into trouble. She hurried to catch him up. "Let me help. If I walk alongside you, I can help keep an eye on things."

Charlie glanced at the man, who was now occupied with unloading cases from another trolley. He shook his head and glanced at Alice's suitcase. "That's a kind offer. But if he saw a passenger helping me—"

"Well...my father works on board, so I'm not really a passenger," interrupted Alice brightly.

Charlie thought for a few seconds, then his cheeks cracked into a grin. "All right then. I am getting behind." The trolley wheels creaked as he set off with it again, this time with Alice walking alongside.

Alice felt a stab of satisfaction at making her own decisions for once, with no teachers telling her what to do or how to behave.

"You're on board the ship with your father for the summer holidays then?" called Charlie.

"Yes," said Alice, feeling a trickle of perspiration inch down her back as she hurried to keep up. A smart tan suitcase wobbled, and Charlie stopped so she could wedge it back into place. She saw him throw an anxious glance at his wristwatch. "How about if we both push the trolley?" she suggested. "It might help balance the luggage and be faster too."

"Only if you're sure," said Charlie.

"I'm quite sure," said Alice with a grin.

"What does your father do?" asked Charlie, as they set off once more. "Let me guess…he's a doctor, or maybe an engineer? No, he's with the Henry Hall Dance Band. Does he play the drums?"

Pushing the trolley with one hand and clutching her suitcase in the other, Alice giggled as Charlie continued to guess her father's profession, but her laughter was stilled by a sudden shout from behind.

"Alice Townsend. What in heaven's name?"

Charlie glanced over his shoulder. "Uh-oh," he said

under his breath, grinding to a halt.

Alice turned to see her father standing a short distance away in his black uniform, his eyes wide in disbelief. She felt a wobble of uncertainty as he strode towards them. The four gold stripes on his lapels and jacket cuffs glinted like a warning.

"Staff Captain Townsend is your father?" gulped Charlie, the colour draining from his cheeks. "But he's in charge of all the crew and the second most important person on the whole ship!"

Chapter 2

THE RACE

Alice had not seen her father for a couple of months and during that time he had grown a trim moustache. If she squinted, it could almost be a stranger standing before her on the dock with his brass-buttoned uniform, polished shoes and wrinkled brow.

"I asked you to wait for me on the train platform, Alice," her father said in an exasperated tone, reaching forward and taking her suitcase.

"I'm sorry. You were late and Charlie needed my help," said Alice, glancing at Charlie, who was chewing on his bottom lip.

Her father's frown deepened as he looked at Charlie. "Why are you helping a porter with his trolley? This really won't do."

"Why not?" Alice asked simply, wiping her damp hands on her skirt.

"Because those are the rules. The crew must not be distracted from their duties," said her father, his eyes narrowing.

"Charlie's trolley was too heavy, and this isn't even his job... He's a bellboy on the lifts – but you might know that already – and some of the luggage almost fell onto some passengers, so I..." explained Alice.

Her father raised a hand, signalling for her to stop talking at once.

Alice met his gaze and thought she detected a hint of amusement dancing behind his eyes, or perhaps that was just her wishful thinking.

"You may return to your duties," her father said to Charlie, in a firm but not unkind way.

Charlie gave him a grateful nod. "Thank you, Staff Captain Townsend. Good day."

"Good luck with the rest of the luggage," Alice called to Charlie.

Charlie gave her a quick wave.

Her father drew in a breath. "You are becoming more like your mother each time I see you."

Alice's stomach flipped over like a pancake. "Am I?" she asked wistfully, hoping for further details she could squirrel away and think over later. Her mother had been working as a ship's seamstress and her father as a junior officer when they had met and married, with Alice born soon after. She had lived with them on board the ship they worked on for the first year of her life, until her mother had died from influenza. Alice wished she could remember her mother and longed to know more about that time, but her father rarely spoke of it.

"Now look, I'm glad you're here, Alice, but if this is to be a success you must follow my instructions. Rules and regulations keep things running smoothly. It's vital you remember that and do not bother the crew," her father said.

She gave him a small nod, feeling a stab of dismay at his obsession with following the rules and his dismissal of the question about her mother.

"I'm sorry I was late," her father continued, leading her towards the crew gangway. "Preparations for our departure in a couple of hours are in full swing and I couldn't get away. The good weather forecast means we have an excellent chance of winning the Blue Riband race on this voyage." He paused and gestured to a porter's wonky bow tie as he walked past. The porter hurriedly straightened it and gave her father a reverential nod.

Alice looked at her father with excitement, remembering the articles she had read about the race in the newspapers. It wasn't a race in the traditional sense of the word – there would be no other ship alongside the *Queen Mary* as she steamed the three thousand nautical miles across the Atlantic. Instead, their ship would be trying to cross the ocean in the fastest time to beat the current record held by another ship – the *Sapphire*.

"Do you really think the *Queen Mary* can beat the *Sapphire*'s record?" asked Alice, following her father onto the gangway and peering over the rail into the oily dock water below. Looking up, she saw her father's jaw twitch. He looked quite determined.

"The captain and I shall make sure she does. This has been my own ambition for a long time, Alice." He paused and looked at her. "If we win, I'm likely to be promoted to captain. That will allow me more shore leave. We'll be able to spend more time together. If you would like that, of course?" He gave her a hopeful smile.

Alice's heart expanded a little. They saw each other so

rarely that she sometimes felt they were like two different species, a tree and a bird perhaps, as they adjusted to one another after being apart. Spending more time together might close that gap. She gave him a shy smile. "Yes. I would like that."

Her father cleared his throat and gave her a brisk nod. "Jolly good. Let's get on board then."

Stepping onto the *Queen Mary*, Alice blinked as her eyes adjusted to the lower light levels. The crew passageway was functional, fat and thin pipes snaking the full length of the ceiling. This was a side of the ship she hadn't seen in newspapers and magazine articles and it was thrilling to discover what went on below deck. The area bustled with activity, as trollies laden with champagne, exotic fresh fruit and seafood packed in ice rattled past. She thought of her meals at boarding school – gristly meat pies, lumpy mashed potato and stodgy puddings. Dinners looked as if they would be a much more delicious experience here and her stomach rumbled in anticipation.

The crew exchanged cheery greetings with one another as they went about their business. Everyone on this passageway had a job to do and knew how to do it, working like cogs in a well-oiled machine.

"Aunt Laura's fall from the ladder was very unfortunate,"

said her father, nodding to another officer as they walked along the passageway. "I spoke with Ipswich Hospital this morning and you'll be pleased to hear her broken leg is not so painful today."

"Poor Aunt Laura. She's always so busy with the orchard and growing her vegetables. She won't like being stuck in bed," said Alice glumly.

After Alice's mother had died, her father's older sister had cared for Alice. With Aunt Laura now injured, Alice had fully expected to be sent home with her best friend Gloria for the first part of the summer holidays, or even to stay on at school with Matron and her two boisterous young sons, for as staff captain, her father was often kept at sea for several months at a time. She had asked numerous times before whether she could visit him on the ships he worked on, but the answer had always been an emphatic "no". So it had been an enormous surprise to be told by her headmistress that, for a few weeks that summer, she would join her father on board the *Queen Mary*, sailing back and forth across the Atlantic until Aunt Laura recovered. Alice wondered, not for the first time, what had changed her father's mind about inviting her on board. Whatever the reason, being here was hugely exciting.

* * *

After taking a lift and a flight of stairs, Alice's father opened a door onto the deck. Alice found herself almost nose to beak with a seagull cruising on the warm currents. It squawked and flew away and she felt a rush of dizziness as she paused and looked over the railing. They were so high up, the people on the dockside were like ants, their cases still being loaded into nets as small as matchboxes.

"Come along," her father urged, unhooking a sign that said *Crew only* across a set of wooden steps.

Alice felt another burst of enjoyment at being allowed somewhere else passengers could not go, and followed him.

"This is Sports Deck," her father said, opening a heavy metal door and ushering her inside. "It's where you'll find the chief officers' cabins and day rooms. I'll be in the wheelhouse, above here, for most of the voyage assisting the captain with safety and navigation. Speaking of which, I must return there now as we prepare to depart."

Alice took her suitcase from her father as he fiddled with a set of brass keys, inserting one into the door marked *Staff Captain*.

"I've had Pearl, the officers' stewardess, make up the small day room for you next to my cabin. There's an internal door linking our rooms and we share a bathroom.

It's saltwater baths only I'm afraid," he said, turning to look at her. He seemed to be weighing his next words carefully. "And you are to stay only on this deck and the one below for the voyage."

Alice was so surprised her suitcase almost slipped from her fingers. "Pardon?"

Her father frowned. "You're the daughter of the staff captain and you're unchaperoned. I'm afraid it wouldn't do for you to mingle with passengers or crew, or roam the ship alone. Seeing you help that porter on the dockside today only confirmed my decision. I have a reputation to uphold, and I must make sure you are safe. You do see that?"

Alice squeezed her hands into fists. "But I was looking forward to seeing Promenade Deck and the shopping parade and going for dinner..." Her voice trailed off as she saw her father's eyes narrow.

"I'm sorry, dear. Those are my rules. I'll have time to give you a tour of the ship when we dock in New York. Now, I've asked Pearl to talk you through the safety drill and show you where to find your lifebelt. Listen to her carefully. Safety at sea is paramount."

Alice swallowed back the tears thickening in her throat. She thought back to earlier in the year when her father had come to visit just before taking up his position on the

Queen Mary. They had sat in a village tearoom eating sticky currant buns as she'd shyly asked him about the new ship, which was billed as the largest, fastest and most luxurious at sea. She'd listened avidly as he'd spoken about the liner's indoor swimming pools, well-appointed staterooms (with their own bathrooms and even toilets that flushed!) and world-class dining saloons where chefs could conjure up whatever food a passenger desired. She'd dreamed of seeing these things one day, and her father had just squashed her wish like an insect under a shoe.

Alice's father gave her a gentle look, perhaps sensing her dismay. "I'll come and see you in a couple of hours after the ship has navigated the Solent. I've left some library books in your cabin. You have brought some other things to occupy you during the long days at sea?" He glanced at his watch.

Alice desperately wanted to protest but could see there was no point in arguing now. He had made up his mind and was clearly in a hurry. "I'd planned to write about our time at sea. I've also brought my embroidery from school."

Her father gave a nod of satisfaction, then turning on the heels of his shiny black shoes, he left her alone in the doorway with only her disappointment for company.

Chapter 3

PEARL

Alice picked up her suitcase and stepped into her father's cabin, the thought that she was forbidden from exploring the ship sitting like a large pebble in her chest. Light from two large portholes shone onto the polished wood-panelled walls and blue carpet. A single bunk with a bedrail lay to the left of the first porthole. From there, the cabin curved gently to the right, the overall shape reminding her of a crescent moon.

A small photograph of Alice on the front steps of her school rested on her father's tidy desk. The image drew her forward and she slumped into his chair. It had been taken in February, on her twelfth birthday. Her father's ship had been in port, and he'd wangled a few hours off to take her out for lunch. But upon his arrival, and much to Alice's dismay, the headmistress had asked him for a "quiet word". She'd known exactly what that "word" would be about.

The previous day, Alice had initiated a game in her dormitory, to see which of the nine girls she shared with could touch the ceiling the most times in one minute by bouncing on their beds. It had ended badly with a broken light fitting and one girl spraining her wrist. Not wanting her friends to get into trouble, Alice had confessed to it being her idea and had suffered two weeks of detentions and no fruit cake after tea as a consequence.

Alice's father had given her a reproachful look after speaking with the headmistress. "Please behave, Alice. Follow the rules and do not get into any more scrapes."

While hating the disappointment in his voice, Alice had found it hard to regret the incident, particularly as the other girls had saved slivers of their own cake for her to enjoy under the covers after lights out.

Pushing thoughts of school away, Alice turned her attention to the other items on her father's desk. Two manifests stamped *Wednesday 22nd July 1936* listed passengers and crew on the voyage, and a leatherbound logbook lay next to them. She flicked through the list of passenger names and cabin numbers, finding it hard to believe this vessel of steel and bolts could carry over three thousand people. Turning her attention to the logbook, she saw it was well-thumbed, and on each page the weather, sea conditions and number of nautical miles travelled were meticulously recorded in her father's neat handwriting. As she examined the book, a small white card fell out. She was about to slip it back inside when the writing on the card made her pause.

HOPE & SON'S NATIONAL DETECTIVE BUREAU.
5th Avenue, New York.
No peace without justice.

Alice frowned. What would her father want with a detective bureau?

"Hello. I take it you are Alice?" said a voice from the door.

Quickly stuffing the card back into the logbook, Alice turned to see a cheerful-looking woman with cherry-red hair and wearing a stewardess uniform. Her smile danced the freckles on her cheeks. "I'm Pearl. I've come to tell you about the safety drill."

"Thank you," said Alice, immediately warming to the stewardess.

Pearl stepped into the cabin and opened an interconnecting door to the right of where Alice was sitting. "Come and see where you'll be sleeping."

Alice stepped over and peered into the small cabin.

"I'm afraid it isn't large, but it has a porthole, so you'll have fresh air," said Pearl.

The cabin was tiny, but comfortable enough. Like her father's, it was wood panelled and smelt pleasantly of polish. There was a small bunk and a chest of drawers below the porthole. It would be a luxury to have her own space after sharing a dorm at school. Outside she could hear shouts from people on the dock, the brass band and the clank of cranes as the ship made its final preparations to depart.

Pearl deftly reached under Alice's bed and pulled out a bulky, white lifebelt. "Once we've set sail, all passengers attend a safety drill, but your father said I should instruct you up here." She went on to show Alice a plan of the ship, told her how to locate the lifeboats and that the ship's whistle would blast seven times in an emergency. "There are some passengers on board who are more interested in having a good time than in safety. But after working on the *Titanic*, I say safety at sea should always be at the forefront of our minds," said Pearl sternly, as she helped Alice stow the lifebelt under her bunk.

Alice's eyes widened. "You were on the *Titanic*? That must have been frightening," she said, recalling her father's stories of the ship striking an iceberg and sinking in the North Atlantic in 1912, almost twelve years before she was born.

Pearl tilted her head to one side. "I was lucky and escaped. I was very afraid, but I couldn't hold on to that fear for ever. Not when being at sea was the only way I knew to make a living."

Alice gave Pearl a shy nod, keen to question her more about life on board the fateful ship but not wanting to appear rude.

"I'm sure you'll enjoy your time here, Alice. There's so much to do and see," Pearl continued as she headed for the door. "I'm sorry I can't stay to talk. There's always such a lot to do on departure day. Your father's left you some library books to keep you busy, although I can't imagine you'll have much time for reading."

Alice stepped over to the stack of books on the chest of drawers. *The Story of Doctor Dolittle. Mary Poppins.* She flicked through the pages which smelled like the school library; a place she did not want to be reminded of just then. She had also already read the books and felt they were a little young for her now.

Alone once more, Alice placed her suitcase on the bed, quickly unpacking her clothes, sandals and washbag, and looked at the three remaining items inside.

With a sigh, she moved her embroidery to one side and pulled her adventures scrapbook from the case. She gave its green cover an affectionate stroke. The adventures inside the book were not her own, but belonged to other people, like aviator Amy Johnson, who had recently regained her record for flying an aeroplane solo all the way from England to South Africa. Alice had avidly followed her journey on the common-room wireless at school. But most of the adventures in the book belonged to her father as he'd travelled the world on different ocean liners. There had been coverage of the *Queen Mary's* maiden voyage, in May, in all the newspapers and Alice had cut out and pasted clippings into her book. She'd hoped this voyage would give her a freedom she often longed for at school and a chance to write about her own adventures. But her words would be limited if she could not explore the ship, and this made her jaw clench in frustration. She gave the third precious item in the case a quick glance, but left it where it was for now.

The ship's engines grumbled and the wall panelling

began to vibrate. They were finally pulling away from the dock. It was the first time she'd been at sea since she was a baby and she did not want to miss a single second of their departure.

Quickly retracing her steps, Alice found a place to stand outside on the curved deck in front of the officers' cabins. Ahead of her the crow's nest reached high into the sky. A man on its observation platform gazed down at the tugs pulling the ship and the flotilla of pleasure boats that had come out to wish the vessel a safe onward voyage. She pulled in a deep breath, the air tangy with salt and oil, as gulls squawked their own noisy farewell.

As they approached the Isle of Wight the wind picked up, whipping Alice's shoulder-length brown hair across her cheeks. They had four full days at sea before arriving in New York early on Monday morning. As she watched the white swells and troughs of the approaching English Channel, she thought again of her father's instructions. Four whole days with nothing but reading and embroidery would be terribly dull. Alice's grip on the varnished handrail tightened as she wondered how she might change her father's mind. Her desire to explore was only increasing with every revolution of the propellors, as the ship steamed towards its destination.

Chapter 4

EXPLORING

Alice woke early the next day, determined to persuade her father to relax his rules, but as soon as she sat up in her bunk a wave of vertigo made her slump back on her pillows. Seasickness. Stomach-churning, saliva-inducing seasickness. Unable to face breakfast – the mere mention of kippers by her father causing her to groan and slam a pillow over her head – she lay still and took deep breaths. This proved difficult with her surroundings pitching and rolling like a never-ending fairground ride.

As her father stood by her bunk, Alice felt the same peculiar awkwardness she'd felt since arriving. Being around him was like wearing a jumper that didn't quite fit. Her father was clearly uncomfortable too as he watched her, stiff-shouldered, but with a look of sympathy straining his cheeks.

Alice swallowed back tears, wishing for a second he was more like her friends' fathers, who dispensed bear-like hugs and fond jokes to their daughters when visiting them at school.

In the end Pearl ushered her father away, saying she would care for Alice and she did so splendidly, arriving every so often with a cooling flannel, fresh peppermint tea and lemon wedges for her to suck on.

To Alice's relief, as the sun began to dip, she started to feel better. And after a bracing saltwater bath, she ventured into her father's cabin to find it quiet. Sitting at his desk, she glanced at the darkening sky through the porthole. To think the whole first day of the voyage had been wasted feeling rotten.

There was a knock at the cabin door, and she was cheered at the sight of Pearl with a dinner tray.

"Good to see the colour back in your cheeks," said Pearl with a grin.

"Yes. Thank you for looking after me," said Alice, smiling too.

"It was no bother at all. I've brought you a light dinner of chicken soup, with peach shortbread for afters," Pearl said, placing down the tray and laying out a set of polished cutlery. "Many folks were suffering like you today. The ship's even been named *Rolling Mary* by some. Anyhow, now you've got used to the motion you'll be able to get out and about tomorrow. You must see the first-class swimming pool and its mother-of-pearl ceiling. The way it shimmers and shines! I sometimes nip in to have a look when no one is around."

"It sounds lovely," said Alice. Pearl clearly didn't know she wasn't allowed to roam the ship and it would be embarrassing to admit the truth.

"Maybe you could even have a swim in there yourself," suggested Pearl, passing Alice a starched napkin. She paused. "I'm afraid your father's got something urgent to attend to and won't be joining you for dinner."

"Is he always this busy?" asked Alice with a frown, smoothing the napkin on her lap. She had banked on persuading her father over dinner that she could be trusted to explore the ship alone and had all her words planned out. She was now twelve and was always (well mostly) on time for lessons at school. She'd even been given the responsibility of changing all the bedsheets in her dorm (it may have been a punishment for being caught eating cake under the covers after lights out, but she didn't *have* to admit that part).

Pearl gave her a sympathetic look. "I'm afraid your father will be busy, especially as the vessel is trying to make the crossing in a record-breaking time. There'll be lots to occupy you on board though, Alice."

While Pearl did some light polishing, turned down the bunks and delivered fresh towels, a slow and steady resolve rose inside Alice as she ate her soup. She could not spend the summer alone, cooped up in this cabin. A day of feeling wretched, along with Pearl's enthusiasm for the ship's swimming pool, had only made her more determined to see the ship for herself. Perhaps, rather than trying to find a moment to persuade her father to change his mind, she could use his long absences to her advantage. If she learned his movements, she might slip away to explore unnoticed and he need never know a thing about it. Her fingers tingled. If she wanted to have her own adventures she would have to break his rules.

The following morning, Alice woke to discover her father had already left for the wheelhouse. His brief note on the breakfast tray, delivered by Pearl, said he would return for lunch at midday. Alice could not prevent a grin from stealing onto her cheeks as she stood looking out of her porthole at the frothy waves and bright sunshine, while wolfing down two slices of toast slathered with honey and a creamy hot chocolate. Her seasickness had not returned, and she was ravenous. With breakfast finished, she hurried outside onto Sun Deck. The air was so clean it was as if it had been freshly washed, and in every direction the ocean swelled and shimmered. The endless space made her feel small but big at the same time. It was quite marvellous.

She noticed a small crowd of people with notepads and cameras huddling round two men who were assembling what looked like a wireless aerial from a bag of equipment labelled *British Broadcasting Company*.

"The people from the BBC are preparing a live wireless broadcast about the race," a lady with a notebook said to Alice as they stood watching. "I've never seen so many journalists and press on board."

"I jolly well hope this vessel wins, as I hear other shipping lines want to steal the trophy away from us," said a man, snapping a picture with his camera.

There was much public interest in the race, and Alice felt a surge of pride at her father's involvement. Seeing that she needed to make the most of her window of opportunity to explore, she quickly made her way to the steps leading to Promenade Deck. If she went down there, there would be no turning back. She would be exploring a part of the ship that was forbidden.

There was a burst of laughter from a couple hurrying towards the same steps. The woman was casually glamorous in her white slacks, red jumper and yellow headscarf. "If you're quick you'll see Fred Astaire – apparently he's tap-dancing on Prom Deck!" she exclaimed to Alice.

Any lingering thoughts of her father and his rules vanished from Alice's head as she heard whoops and claps spilling up from the deck below. Fred Astaire, the actor! She and her friend Gloria had so enjoyed seeing his film *Top Hat* at the pictures last year. He and the actress Ginger Rogers had been wonderful together.

Hurrying down the steps after the two passengers, Alice's eyes widened. The immense size of the ship was brought into sharp focus by the rectangular pools of light reflecting from the windows onto the teak deck. Steamer chairs and small tables sat in regimented rows, stretching the full length of the vessel, allowing a path for those passengers taking a morning walk.

Alice's eyes were drawn past all of this to a small, excited crowd gathered in front of a window. Above their heads she caught a glimpse of Fred Astaire in a dapper grey suit, balancing on the railing against the glass and doing a gentle jig in his tap shoes. It was the most bizarre and wonderful thing she had ever seen. She thought of her adventures scrapbook, her fingers already itching to record every detail of seeing a real-life actor here, on her father's ship.

Tipping his hat, Fred sprang from the railing and gave a small bow to his audience.

Flashbulbs popped as the ship's photographers recorded the moment.

Alice shrank back a little. It would not do to be included in any of those photographs. Imagine if her father saw! Throwing Fred Astaire one final glance, she hurried on past the crowd, noticing that everywhere she looked people were dressed in their finest clothes, with elegantly styled hair, and women with red-painted lips and nails the order of the day. Alice glanced down briefly at her own navy slacks, cream cardigan and sandals. She remembered her father saying that stewards could always tell what class a person was travelling in from the clothes they were wearing. He had told her of stewards being offered bribes from passengers in third and second class in exchange for a chance to explore parts of the ship that were out of bounds to them. Her own clothes were not smart, but they would have to do. Anyhow, no one seemed to be paying her any attention.

At a set of double doors, Alice stood back as a woman in an extravagant red hat with black feathers emerged with a wave of heavy perfume that made her nose itch. She was closely followed by a maid wearing a frilled cap and carrying three large shopping bags.

Stepping through the doors herself, Alice found herself in the shopping arcade. The warm varnished woods, shimmering bronze shop frontages displaying books, clothes and souvenirs, and russet red pillars and green marble effect flooring gave this place a sumptuous air. It certainly rivalled the shops Alice had seen on a rare visit to central London with her aunt last year. She turned and glimpsed the sparkling sea through the glass doors. It was remarkable that this was all happening miles from land – and to think her father had not wanted her to experience it!

The brief glimmer of guilt she felt at disobeying her father slipped away, as she looked in W.H. Smith & Son booksellers at puzzle books, souvenir handkerchiefs and tourist guides to New York. A stand of writing pens caught her eye, but she had no money and needed to move on. She had to see the whole ship in case this was her only opportunity. She knew, from studying plans of the ship stuck in her adventures scrapbook, that there were twelve decks. The first-class swimming pool – with the beautiful ceiling Pearl had spoken of – was on D Deck, five below where she was now.

She headed for the nearest stairwell, keeping her head low. The flow of passengers lessened as she worked her way down, everyone wanting to be on the upper decks, making the most of the shops, public rooms, deck space and beautiful weather.

A uniformed officer strode up the stairs towards her with a clipboard. Alice stiffened, worried she was about to be discovered, but he carried on without giving her a second look. She didn't know him, and there was no reason he would know her either. This was the first time she had travelled with her father, and she had not met anyone aside from the steward who had bumped into her on the quayside, the bellboy and Pearl. Her shoulders relaxed as she realized she was safe, for now.

Emerging onto D Deck alone, she stood and listened to the sounds of laughter spilling down the stairwell and the gentle creaks of the wooden panelling as the ship rolled like an elegant lady at a dance. The half-moon entrance to the first-class swimming pool lay straight ahead. She saw with dismay a wooden sign in front of the doors indicating that the pool was closed and would remain so for another forty-five minutes.

Stepping round the sign, Alice stood on tiptoes to look through the glass in the upper part of the door, hoping for a glance of the special ceiling. To her surprise, as she leaned against the door to steady herself it opened a little. *It was unlocked.* Glancing around and seeing no one was looking, she smiled to herself and slipped inside.

Chapter 5

ARGUMENT

Alice's jaw dropped as she took in the sight of the first class swimming pool. It rose to twice the height of the other decks, with straw-coloured tiles, interspersed with bands of emerald and crimson, and grand columns that rose up and up. She tipped her head to look at the ceiling and gasped. It was as magnificent as Pearl had implied. The mother-of-pearl tiles glistened, reflections from the water scattering waves of light across them. It was mesmerizing and quite the most fantastic pool Alice had ever seen.

A double staircase behind the pool's diving board led

to a balcony and changing cubicles. Even though it was against the rules, she had an itch to explore further, and Alice made her way up the stairs, watching the water in the pool moving rhythmically in time with the ship's movement. She imagined the shrieks of amusement as people jumped from the diving board. She was not a strong swimmer herself. She'd been put off the sport after years of being forced to use her school's unheated swimming pool on even the coldest of days. But she could see there was a lot of fun to be had in here.

Her thoughts were interrupted by the clunk of the pool door opening.

Alice glanced at her watch. It was another half-hour before the pool opened to passengers. Perhaps a member of the crew had come to get things ready. It would not do to be caught be in here. Making a quick decision, she opened the door of the nearest changing cubicle, ducked inside and quietly slipped the lock across. Sitting on the wooden bench, she tucked in her feet so they would not be visible under the gap in the door, her heart racing. She listened quietly as footsteps echoed off the tiles. The person was following the route she had taken, up the stairs to the balcony and towards the cubicles.

Alice felt a prickle of unease at being discovered, as she

heard the entrance door opening and closing again. She hugged her knees to her chest. *A second person had come in.*

The footsteps on the balcony paused. "Why are you here? Did you follow me?" she heard someone say with alarm. It sounded like a young man and he was close by, just a short distance from where she was hiding.

Alice bit hard on her bottom lip, feeling a rush of anxiety.

"I had to follow you. What have you done with it?" the second person demanded. It was another man, but he sounded older and spoke with a clipped British accent.

"I won't help you," said the younger man. Alice felt he was trying to be brave, but the wobble in his voice betrayed his true feelings.

"We had an arrangement," said the older man curtly. The sound of his feet thumping up the stairs to the balcony made Alice shrink back against the wall of the cubicle. She'd stumbled into something she wasn't meant to, and now there was no way out.

"What about the Pig and Whistle?" the older man asked, his voice closer now.

"I told you. I've changed my mind about taking it. Please. You need to stop this," said the younger man. His voice was cracked and very fearful.

There was a short pause and the air seemed to crackle with tension.

"If you're not going to do as we agreed, then return the package to me. Now!" the older man persisted.

Alice's heart hammered against her ribs; she was deeply regretting her decision to explore.

"No," said the young man, his voice wobbling. "I'll...I'll tell someone what you're doing," he said desperately.

Footsteps rushed forward. "You'll say nothing, do you hear?" growled the older man.

"Please don't hurt me...please..." begged the young man.

Alice gripped her knees harder.

"You leave me no choice," growled the older man.

There was a sharp and high intake of breath from the younger man, followed by a heavy *thud-thud-thud-thud-thud.* It sounded like something, or someone, was falling. There was a sickening pause, then all Alice could hear was the water sloshing in the pool and the juddery vibrations of the ship.

Alice leaned forward, every muscle in her body tense and alert. The wooden bench she was sitting on creaked, breaking the silence.

"Who's there?" she heard the older man say sharply.

Alice held her breath, black spots dancing in front of her eyes. There was another long pause, then to her relief she heard the older man's footsteps hurrying away and the door to the swimming pool quietly opening and closing.

Alice waited.

And waited.

And waited.

Her mouth was bone dry as she listened for something to indicate the younger man was leaving too. But that confirmation didn't come, and she had a horrible feeling she knew why.

She unlocked the cubicle door and slowly pushed it open. Creeping along the balcony, she clamped a hand to her lips as she reached the top of the staircase. At the foot of the steps lay a pale-faced young man in a white uniform. His eyes were closed.

With a jolt of recognition Alice saw it was Joseph Wilks, the steward who had bumped into her on the dockside two days before. As she ran down the steps, she saw his wonky name badge was straight now, but his head wasn't. It lay at an awkward angle, while a crimson flush slowly stained the straw-coloured tiles around his hair, turning them an awful red.

Chapter 6

HELP

Alice swallowed a scream as she stood looking at Joseph's limp body. The thuds as he fell down the stairs sat heavy in her head. Trying to make sense of the scene before her, she thought of the last words the steward had said, and the undisguised fear in his voice. *"Please don't hurt me."*

Kneeling beside him, she tentatively placed a hand on his chest. He was still breathing. Alice's own heart beat strongly in response. "Hello. Can you hear me?" she whispered, throwing an anxious glance to the pool entrance. What if the man with the clipped voice returned?

A rash of goosebumps needled her arms, as water sloshed over the edges of the pool.

"Please wake up," Alice pleaded, giving Joseph a gentle shake. He didn't respond and his eyes remained firmly shut. She could feel his breathing becoming shallower by the second. She had to get help, and quickly – there was no other option, even if it meant leaving him for a brief minute. She sprang to her feet at the same time as the door to the pool swung open.

To Alice's relief, a woman wearing a silky blue robe and carrying a towel stepped inside.

"Help...please help," Alice called, her voice tinny.

The woman gasped and hurried over. "Oh!" she exclaimed, her towel dropping to the tiles as she took in the scene before her.

"He needs a doctor," said Alice urgently, bending to feel Joseph's chest again. His heart felt worryingly weak beneath her palm.

"There's a telephone by the pool entrance," said the woman, whose face had turned ashen. "I'll call the ship's hospital right away."

Alice gave the woman a grateful nod.

The woman returned quickly. "The doctor is coming," she said, kneeling beside Alice and resting a caring hand on her arm. She glanced at the water swilling around the tiles. "When I swam in here on a previous voyage I almost slipped myself; it's quite dangerous when water spills over the side of the pool."

The woman was assuming Joseph had slipped and fallen, but Alice wasn't at all sure that was what had happened. She opened her mouth to correct the woman as the door to the pool opened again. Peering over the top of the diving board Alice saw a boy, perhaps only a couple of years older than she was. He had thick brown hair and his eyebrows pulled together as he scanned the pool area. He was looking for someone.

The woman stood up and looked at the boy. "I'm afraid there's been a dreadful accident. The doctor's been called."

"An accident?" repeated the boy, his forehead creasing.

"Yes. A steward by the name of Joseph Wilks," said the woman, looking down at Joseph's name badge.

The boy looked stricken, and a flash of fear crossed his face. He slowly backed through the door and disappeared.

Alice's brief flutter of suspicion at the boy's reaction was swallowed by a flurry of activity as the doctor and nurse arrived, followed by two orderlies with a stretcher. She stood well back as they set about tending to Joseph, her arms wrapped round her middle in an endeavour to stop the shivers rising up her legs. The doctor would discover who she was if she spoke to him and might tell her father, but something terrible had happened and she needed to tell someone.

The woman in the robe introduced herself as Mrs Cuthbert and chattered away to the doctor, gesturing again at the stairs and the water sloshing above the rim of the pool.

"The patient's breathing is erratic. We must transfer him to the hospital at once," said the doctor to the nurse in a low voice. He turned to Mrs Cuthbert. "I shall make a note in the accident report that the steward slipped and that you found him. I'm afraid swimming pools can be quite a hazard at sea when the ship is rocking back and forth."

Alice's hands felt clammy. This wasn't a slip or a casual fall, it was more than that. And Mrs Cuthbert hadn't found Joseph, *she* had.

Mrs Cuthbert sniffed and pulled the belt of her robe tighter. "More should be done to contain the water in the pool."

The doctor took Joseph's pulse while the nurse wrapped a bandage round his head. "I'm afraid nothing can be done, Mrs Cuthbert. We are at sea and at the mercy of the waves." He beckoned the orderlies over. "Please transfer the patient to the stretcher and take him to the hospital. Be careful to keep his head and neck stable."

Alice sidled closer to the doctor, preparing to tell him what she had overheard. Joseph had been pushed by the older man; she was sure of it.

"I think that young girl wants to speak with you," said Mrs Cuthbert, peering at Alice. "Oh dear. She looks very pale."

The doctor glanced at Alice. "Why are you still here? You can go now, dear. It's all in hand."

Alice felt a flash of irritation at the doctor's dismissive tone. "But...I need to tell you what..." she began, but the doctor wasn't listening. His attention was once more on Mrs Cuthbert, who was asking why the ship couldn't be slowed down at certain times of the day to make swimming less hazardous, and could this request please be put to the captain.

"Mrs Cuthbert, I'm afraid I must stop you there. I need to get this young man to the hospital at once. He's unconscious and in a bad way," said the doctor, clearly irritated now.

"Please...may I say something," said Alice, willing the doctor to listen to everything she had overheard while hiding in the cubicle.

The doctor turned, his eyes narrowing. "I really have no time to speak to you now. Mrs Cuthbert here will escort you back to your cabin and see that you get some sweet tea. It's good for shock." He said these words as if Alice were a delicate flower in danger of wilting in the slightest of breezes.

The doctor's condescending attitude made something flare deep inside Alice, for she did not consider herself delicate at all, not when she endured weekly three-mile cross-country runs at school, once twisting her ankle and hobbling to the finish through melting snow.

Her cheeks hot with indignation, Alice watched now as the orderlies, doctor and nurse hurried Joseph away on the stretcher. His eyes were closed and his cheeks were deathly pale. Joseph needed help and she saw it would be wrong to delay the doctor further by trying to make him listen.

Mrs Cuthbert took Alice's arm. "Well. That was a horrid and unexpected start to the day. Let me escort you to your cabin like the doctor asked."

"Oh no. That's quite all right," said Alice, quickly unhooking her arm. The last thing she needed was Mrs Cuthbert talking with her father.

Mrs Cuthbert frowned and reached for Alice's arm again. "I'm not sure I should leave you alone..." she fussed.

Alice did not wait to hear the rest of her sentence. Twisting away from Mrs Cuthbert, she hurried through the door and headed for the stairs she had come down only a short while ago. She looked around anxiously, suddenly afraid that the man who had been speaking with Joseph might be waiting in the shadows.

Rushing up the stairs and arriving on the first landing, Alice saw with surprise the boy who had briefly made an appearance at the pool. He was standing by a potted fern, its soft fronds gently waving as the ship steamed on.

"Keep going up. She's following you," he whispered.

Alice looked over her shoulder. Mrs Cuthbert *was* coming after her. Giving the boy a grateful nod, Alice sped up, taking the stairs two at a time. Upon reaching the B Deck stairwell, she stood and peered through the gap to the decks below, her heart pounding as she caught her breath.

"Yes. I saw the girl. She went along the C Deck passageway," she heard the boy say, giving her a chance to get away.

"Jolly good. Thank you," Mrs Cuthbert replied.

A few seconds later the boy arrived in front of her, pink-faced and also out of breath.

"Thank you for helping," said Alice gratefully.

The boy smiled, then his face became serious. "Actually, I was waiting for you. I wanted to speak with you about Joseph." He took a step closer. "I know Joseph. He asked to meet me this morning at the pool, but...I was late."

Alice frowned. How could this boy know the steward well enough to arrange a meeting? They had been on board the ship for less than two days.

"You were with Joseph when I came into the swimming pool. What happened in there?" the boy continued. His brow furrowed with anxiety.

Alice stared at him, then glanced around. Mrs Cuthbert might come back, and she needed to stay hidden from her father. Then there was the man who had argued with Joseph and the terrible thing she thought he had done. She felt the onset of tears building in her throat. The bravery she had been clinging onto was rapidly slipping away. She pressed her heels into the carpet until the tightness in her throat eased. "I can't talk here," she whispered.

The boy gave her a searching look. "Do you like animals?"

"I suppose so. My aunt keeps hens," said Alice, thinking that was a peculiar question.

The boy's face softened, as if this answer pleased him. "I know somewhere on Sun Deck. We can go and talk there. My name's Sonny, by the way."

"I'm Alice," she replied.

Sonny gestured for her to follow him and, as Alice watched him bound up the steps, she saw again in her mind a vision of Joseph unconscious at the bottom of the stairs. She did not want to be alone after the troubling events of the morning. If this boy knew Joseph, she wondered if he could help with the worrying questions that were building up by the minute. With once last quick look around, she lowered her head and hurried after him.

Chapter 7

KENNELS

Two windswept men hooted with laughter as they threw a small woven circle of rope back and forth across a low-slung net, while two women looked on in amusement. Life on board was continuing as normal, yet as Alice followed Sonny along the port side of Sun Deck, she didn't feel normal at all. The sun was bright and warm and the sea swell slight, but Alice felt shivery remembering Joseph's sharp intake of breath as he fell, and the echo of the other man's footsteps as he ran away.

Arriving at a metal door in the wall, Sonny rang a bell to one side. The sound of yaps and barks came from inside.

"We're at the dog kennels," said Alice. She had stuck a photograph of dogs being walked along the deck in her adventures scrapbook. Wealthy passengers often travelled with their pampered pets, demanding only the best care and attention.

"I help walk the dogs from time to time. I find it's a good place to think," said Sonny. "Sometimes tired seabirds land on the ship and crew bring them up here to recover. Last week we had a young Arctic tern. Did you know they migrate all the way from the Arctic to the Antarctic each year?" he continued.

"Goodness," said Alice, seeing that Sonny looked quite animated. "You've travelled on this ship before then?"

"I've been on the *Queen Mary* for almost three months now, with my governess Dorothy," Sonny said, his face falling a little as the dogs continued to yap.

Alice swallowed her surprise. That was a long time to be at sea, but it also explained how he knew Joseph well enough to arrange a meeting.

A man in green overalls opened the door; his name badge was marked *Kennel Master*. "Morning, Sonny," he said with a welcoming grin. "Come to visit our canine passengers again? You've bought a friend this time too."

"You don't mind?" asked Sonny, glancing at Alice.

"Not at all. We've got five dogs on this westbound voyage. Three poodles with peculiar haircuts, a yappy Pekinese and a rather fetching chap who looks more wolf than dog, but he's friendly enough. Excuse me while I cut up the steak for the poodles' lunch," said the kennel master. "It's been ordered in by their owner from Harrod's Food Hall in London and I'm almost tempted to eat it myself!" With a grin he disappeared into a side room and the sound of a knife on a chopping board could soon be heard.

Alice followed Sonny onto an enclosed area of deck. In the centre sat a small black lamp post. It was the kind of thing you saw on a street or in a park and it looked very out of place.

Sonny saw Alice looking at it. "The lamp post was put in after the King of England travelled on board with his dogs. He said it would make his pets feel more at home when they went about their business."

Alice shook her head in amazement. The ship really did go above and beyond in its efforts to keep its passengers happy.

In roomy wire enclosures adjacent to the deck, the dogs barked a greeting to the two children. Giving them a fond glance, Sonny led Alice to a wooden bench in the sun. The animals began to settle, the three poodles lying down together in a corner while the white wolf-dog and the Pekinese sniffed at each other through the bars.

Sitting down, Sonny turned to face Alice and she saw his jaw was firm, giving his face a purposeful look. "Joseph asked to meet me this morning to discuss a problem he had. I can't believe he had an accident before I arrived. Did you see what happened?"

Alice ran a finger down the armrest of the bench, which was sticky with salt spray. She swallowed nervously, wondering how much to say. Sonny was clearly concerned for his friend and her instinct was to trust him. "My father's the staff captain. He doesn't want me exploring the ship, but I did anyway." She paused, seeing Sonny's eyes widen like saucers. She went on to tell him about taking a look in the swimming pool while it was closed and hiding in a cubicle after someone came in. She paused again, the memory of the *thud-thud-thud* of Joseph's falling body echoing in her ears.

"Go on," encouraged Sonny gently.

"I think Joseph came up to the balcony first. Then an older man arrived. They had an argument. Joseph said he would tell someone what the man had been doing. That's when things changed. The man wasn't happy at all. Joseph was scared and asked the man not to hurt him," said Alice.

Sonny sucked on his teeth.

"The man said Joseph had left him with no choice. I think he pushed Joseph down the steps," said Alice.

Sonny sat back in the bench. "But he could have killed Joseph. Is that what he wanted, do you think?"

The words sat between them, as thick and weighty as a slab of concrete.

Alice wiped her suddenly sweaty palms on her slacks.

Sonny swallowed. "Joseph has been acting strangely for a few weeks. I asked him what was wrong, and he said a passenger had requested a favour. He'd agreed, but then decided to back out of it. He was going to tell me more today."

"You think the man Joseph argued with could be this passenger?" asked Alice.

"Perhaps," said Sonny, as he watched the wolf-dog lick the Pekinese's nose through the bars.

"If you don't mind me asking, why did Joseph choose to talk to you about his problem?" said Alice, thinking it a bit odd for a member of the ship's crew to confide in a passenger.

"Fair question," said Sonny with a nod. "Dorothy wanted me to improve my swimming. I was allowed to join the crew's lessons after hours and Joseph and I hit it off."

He paused and rubbed his nose. "When Joseph told me he had a problem I suggested he speak with his supervisor, but he said he couldn't. That made me see it must be serious."

"I saw Joseph on the dock," Alice said, telling Sonny how harassed the steward had looked when he bumped into her.

Sonny looked glum. "If I hadn't been late, I might have stopped this from happening. The thought that someone wanted to kill him is sickening. He looked awful when the orderlies carried him off to the hospital."

Alice gripped her knees as she remembered Joseph's head wound. "I tried to tell the doctor what I thought had happened, but he wouldn't listen. He and Mrs Cuthbert – that's the woman who was in there – thought it was an accident and Joseph had slipped and fallen. If it had been an accident surely the other man would have stayed to help, rather than running off."

Sonny stood up. "I agree. But we'll only learn who did this from Joseph himself."

"But he was knocked unconscious by the fall," said Alice.

"We have to hope he wakes up," said Sonny determinedly, pacing round the lamp post.

"But what if the man who hurt him tries to hurt someone else?" said Alice, a cord of panic constricting her chest.

Sonny stepped over to the dogs' enclosure and kneeled in front of it. The wolf dog came trotting over. "You didn't see the man Joseph was talking with, but you did hear him? Do you think you'd recognize his voice if you heard it again?"

Alice frowned. "Perhaps. But how would I do that? There must be thousands of men on board," she said, walking over to the enclosure too.

"True. But there has to be some way we can identify him," said Sonny with a frown.

Alice crouched beside Sonny and thought hard, hoping to remember something useful. "There is something," she said. "The man asked Joseph what he'd done with a package. He seemed awfully keen to get it back. He mentioned something about a pig and whistle too, whatever that means."

Sonny looked up. "The Pig and Whistle? That's the name of the crew's pub on board this ship." The wolf-dog pressed his side against the wall of the cage and Sonny reached through the wire and rubbed his neck. "I wonder what could be inside this package?"

The thought hit Alice square between the eyebrows. "If Joseph was refusing to give the package to the man, maybe it's still on board?"

Sonny looked at her thoughtfully. "Gosh. You could be right."

"If we find it, it might lead us to the person who hurt him," suggested Alice.

"You think *we* should look for this package?" asked Sonny, his nose wrinkling.

Alice shrugged as the Pekinese came over and sniffed her hand. "It's an idea."

Sonny looked worried. "I don't know about this, Alice. The man who pushed Joseph is dangerous. We should tell someone."

"But we don't have any evidence or clue as to who he is. Who will believe us?" said Alice. She leaned forward. "And what if he *does* do something like this again and nothing has been done to stop him?" She felt hot at this terrible thought. "The ship docks in three days. We must find the culprit by then."

Sonny's jaw twitched. "You're right. We need to do something."

"Could Joseph have hidden the package in his cabin?" asked Alice.

"Joseph shares a cabin. I'll ask one of his roommates to have a look around. We could meet up later to see if he finds anything," suggested Sonny.

Alice nodded, the urgent need to get justice for Joseph flaring through her. This was a far more worthy pursuit than working on her embroidery or waiting for her father to appear. A crime had been committed and they needed to get to the bottom of it.

Chapter 8

THE GLOVE

Alice slipped into her cabin as a single blast of the ship's whistle marked midday. Her father's cabin was quiet; his work must have delayed him again. Quickly brushing the tangles from her hair, she caught a glimpse of her suitcase under her bed. Sliding it out and opening it, she picked up her adventures scrapbook and a sharpened pencil. Sitting cross-legged on the bunk, she turned to a new page and jotted down everything that had happened that morning. She made a careful note of the argument between Joseph and the man in the swimming pool; it might come in useful later.

Returning the book to her case, she looked at the item folded up next to it – her most precious possession. The dove-grey silk glove embroidered with intertwining peach-coloured roses stared back at her. She lifted it out and slipped it onto her right hand. She had discovered the glove swaddled beneath her aunt's winter jumpers in a trunk in the attic, while searching for a board game during the Easter holidays. Inside the glove, embroidered in cobalt thread, were her mother's initials. R.T. *Rose Townsend.* She had shown the glove to her aunt, whose face had softened.

"Your father gave away your mother's belongings soon after she died. I think they were too painful a reminder. I found this glove in one of your father's trunks and decided to keep it safe. I felt it important to keep something of your mother's to pass on to you when you were older," her aunt had said a little guiltily.

"But where is the other glove?" Alice had asked.

Her aunt shook her head wistfully. "It must be lost I'm afraid."

Alice often quietly observed her friends' mothers arriving at the start and end of each school term, their kisses and hugs dispensed as easily as penny sweets. It made Alice wonder if she missed her own mother, but she concluded it was hard to miss someone you'd never known. It was strange, though, because the older she got, the more she *thought* she missed her mother, and this brought an unexpected ache to her chest.

The sound of voices in the passageway caught Alice's attention. She quickly returned the glove to the suitcase and tidied it away, then crept to the door, pressing her ear hard against it.

"We must transfer Joseph to a hospital as soon as we arrive in New York if he's to survive," said a voice. It was the doctor!

Alice bit hard on her lower lip at hearing his words.

"What a terrible business. Please ensure Joseph's family are informed and told of the seriousness of his injury," she heard her father reply. "He should have been working this morning. It's a puzzle why he was at the swimming pool at that time."

"Hmm," said the doctor. "That is peculiar."

"Did he have anything on his person to explain why he was there?" asked Alice's father.

"No. Only his cabin keys. I suspect we won't know the circumstances until he wakes up... *if* he wakes up," said the doctor grimly.

Alice drew in a sharp breath at hearing the doubt in the doctor's voice.

"Anyhow, here is the accident report with all the details. If you could sign and return it to me later that would be helpful," continued the doctor.

"Of course. Thank you," said Alice's father. "I shall also send a personal message of support to Joseph's family. Our paths have crossed before and he's a likeable chap."

Alice stood away from her door, feeling sick at the grim news that Joseph might not wake up. When she met Sonny later, she would have to tell him things were looking very bad indeed for his friend.

The ice cubes in Alice's freshly squeezed lemonade clinked in time with the ship's vibrations. Her appetite vanished as her father spoke over lunch about how they were barrelling along at twenty-nine knots and had set a new record of 760 nautical miles, across the last stretch. But all Alice could think of was Joseph and how poorly he was. Investigating what had happened to him now seemed vaguely ridiculous. She and Sonny were only children after all. Perhaps she should tell her father, but she wasn't sure he would believe her and look in to what happened himself. There was also the problem that if he found out she had disobeyed him he would pay closer attention to her whereabouts.

That meant she would no longer be able to investigate the crime with Sonny.

It was a dilemma Alice didn't know how to solve.

Her father suddenly placed his fork down and reached for Alice's hands. His grip was firm and warm. "I'm sorry, dear. Am I boring you?"

"Um...no," said Alice, but her father's lopsided smile made her think her words weren't convincing enough.

"Thank you for following my instructions to stay on the upper decks. I realize you are disappointed, but you've accepted it without complaint. That's very grown up of you," he said, giving her hands a squeeze.

Guilt swirled in Alice's stomach, and she stared at her plate.

"I hope we can spend more time together after this voyage, but the race for the trophy means I currently have little time for anything else. You do see how important this is for my promotion? Everything must run smoothly. There can be no dramas or distractions."

Alice nodded.

Her father leaned forward. "I would like to see the needlework keeping you occupied on this voyage. Might you show it to me?"

Fetching her embroidery, Alice placed it in his hands,

thankful he hadn't asked to see it before now as he would realize how little progress she had made on the voyage.

Her father examined the half-sewn map of the British Isles with surprise. "I must say I was expecting to see a floral arrangement, or a bird perhaps. But this map...it's tremendous, Alice." He traced a finger over a sailing boat with a red sail off the Suffolk coast. "I think your mother would have liked it too."

Alice felt a glow of warmth. "Did Mother enjoy working as a seamstress on ships? You hardly ever speak of that time."

Her father's eyes looked a little watery. He folded the cloth and passed it back to Alice. "We were all very happy living at sea together for a while." A flash of worry tightened his cheeks, as if this conversation was a dark path he didn't want to venture down.

The telephone on the desk gave a shrill ring. Failing to hide his relief at the interruption, her father picked it up and listened intently. "That was important. I'm afraid I must go," he said after the call was finished. "I'll ask Pearl to prepare you a dinner tray. I'm likely to be very late so please don't wait up again. I'll see you in the morning, dear." Giving her a quick pat on the shoulder, he shrugged on his jacket and hurried back to his duties in the wheelhouse.

The flash of companionship they had shared just then had been like being bathed in golden sunlight and Alice found she was hungry for more. She was also hungry to solve the mystery of what had happened to Joseph and did not want her father to put a stop to their investigations. Chewing on her lower lip, she looked at her father's desk. She had seen him slip a sheet of paper into the drawer when she had come in for lunch; it must have been the accident report the doctor had given him for signing. It might contain something to help them in their investigation – and if there was anywhere to start, it was there.

Chapter 9

ACCIDENT REPORT

CREW ACCIDENT REPORT

<u>Date</u>: Friday 24ᵗʰ July 1936.

<u>Time of incident</u>: 0900 hours

<u>Name</u>: Joseph Wilks

<u>Occupation</u>: Cabin Steward: Cabins A80–99

<u>Location of incident</u>: D Deck: First-Class
Swimming Pool

<u>Injury</u>: Head wound. Unconscious – condition
serious and deteriorating

<u>Cause</u>: Wet tiles caused him to slip

<u>Logged by</u>: Doctor T. Phillips

REMARKS:

Found by Mrs Cuthbert (cabin B25) there for an early swim.

Young female passenger at the scene. No comments made.

Query why Joseph was in pool area at time of accident when he should have been on cabin duty.

As Alice read the accident report, she puffed out a small breath of irritation at the doctor's second remark, which she presumed was a reference to her. *No comments made.* If the doctor had taken a moment to listen, he might have found her comments very useful indeed. She saw there was no indication that Joseph's fall had been anything other than an accident and she frowned as she read the doctor's third remark for a second time. It did seem a little curious that Joseph had asked to meet Sonny in the pool area. Why that particular place?

Carefully returning the report, Alice tried to push the drawer closed, but something was obstructing one of the sliders. She glanced at the door, hoping that Pearl wouldn't choose this moment to come in and clear away the lunch things. It wouldn't do to be caught snooping.

Reaching inside the drawer, her fingers grasped a piece

of twine. She tugged it free and saw it was attached to a white luggage tag for the *Queen Mary*'s hold, along with three brass keys. They were the type that would fit a lock on a suitcase or trunk. The wording on the tag indicated three trunks were stored in row twelve of the forward hold. But also attached to the twine was an older, frayed luggage tag.

Alice sat back in the chair with a whump as she read the name on it.

Rose Townsend.

Her mother.

What did this mean? Were those her mother's trunks in the hold? Aunt Laura had clearly said that Alice's father had given away her mother's possessions. Glancing towards her cabin, Alice thought of the silk glove hidden inside her own suitcase. Could the matching glove be here, on the *Queen Mary*? She felt a squeeze in her chest.

Carefully and regretfully returning the tags and keys to the drawer, Alice thought again of the *Hope & Son's National Detective Bureau* card hidden in the pages of her father's logbook. Her father was keeping secrets, and it made her tingle with curiosity. Did she dare take the keys and search the hold for answers? The thought was tantalizing, but she needed to put it to one side for now and first and foremost help get justice for Joseph.

*   *   *

"I know you," the bellboy said to Alice a little after five o'clock that afternoon, as the three children stood in an alcove close to a crew door on D Deck. "You're Alice. The staff captain's daughter."

"Hello again, Charlie," said Alice, both surprised and delighted to find he was one of Joseph's roommates. Today Charlie wore a smart red jacket with brass buttons, shiny black shoes and an oval brimless hat that looked a little like a drum. He undid the strap holding the hat in place and took it off, grinning as Sonny looked on in amazement.

"How do you and Alice know each other?" asked Sonny.

"Alice helped me on the dockside – well – until her father arrived," said Charlie with a cheeky smile.

"I hope you didn't get into trouble," said Alice with a grimace.

Charlie's eyes twinkled and he shrugged. "Nothing I couldn't handle." The light in his eyes dimmed and he looked both ways along the passageway, which curved upwards towards the bow and stern. "I felt bad poking around in Joseph's things, but I didn't find any package in our cabin," he said, his voice low. "We've regular cabin inspections, so I doubt he would've hidden something important in there anyway. It must be somewhere else."

Sonny made a small noise of frustration.

"There's something I need to tell you about Joseph," said Alice, and she updated the two boys on everything she'd overheard the doctor say about their friend's deteriorating condition and the accident report she had sneaked a look at.

"The thought that someone hurt my friend makes my blood boil," said Charlie fiercely, jamming his hat back on his head and adjusting the chinstrap. "We must find out who did this. Joseph's father left to start a new life in Australia a few months back. Joseph gives most of his wages to his mum and two younger brothers." Charlie paused, his eyes suddenly hazy. "He's made his youngest brother a model of the *Queen Mary* out of matchsticks for his birthday next month. It's the cleverest thing I've ever seen. But what if...?"

There was a moment of silence as Charlie's unspoken words hung over them like a dark cloud. Joseph sounded kind and caring. It would be a tragedy if he didn't survive to see his family again.

Sonny turned to Alice, his face pale. "Did you learn anything else from the doctor or the report that might help us? You are quite good at this detective lark."

Alice thought back. "There was something. The accident

report questioned why Joseph was in the pool area. He had arranged to meet you there, Sonny. But why choose that place?"

Sonny frowned. "Now I think of it, why not ask to meet me in the A-Deck stewards' room instead? It would have been closer for both of us, and more private. He was very insistent it had to be the pool."

The vessel was listing more than earlier, and Alice reached for the roped handrail to steady herself, still thankful her seasickness hadn't returned. "When I was hiding in the changing cubicle Joseph came directly up to the balcony. Why did he not just wait for Sonny by the pool entrance? Unless…" She paused, her brain whirring.

"What are you thinking?" asked Charlie, staring at her.

The rope weave prickled Alice's palm as the thought took shape. "Joseph didn't have the package with him this morning, but what if he had hidden it somewhere on the balcony and wanted to show it to Sonny when he arrived?"

Sonny's eyes widened with understanding. "Now that's an idea."

Charlie grinned at Alice. "Nice work, Sherlock Holmes."

Alice felt a warm glow at the praise. "There's no time to lose. We must go and search for the package at once."

Chapter 10

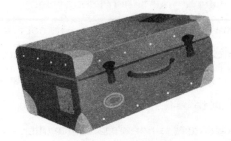

WATCHED

Sonny glanced at his wristwatch as he, Alice and Charlie stood in the passageway. "The swimming pool is usually quiet at this time as everyone is getting dressed for dinner. I agree with Alice, we should look for the package now."

Charlie glanced at the crew door. "I'm not supposed to be in passenger areas unless I'm working. He looked down at his clothes. "I suppose I'm in my uniform though. I could say I'm helping with directions if anyone asks. Let's talk as we walk. It will look less suspicious."

Sonny nodded. "The quickest route to the pool is this way," he said, turning and gesturing for Charlie and Alice to follow him towards the front of the ship. "Dorothy is expecting me at dinner, so we'd better hurry." He looked to Alice. "What about your father? I don't want you to get into any trouble."

"Pearl, his stewardess, is leaving me a dinner tray. My father's very busy with the Blue Riband race, so I shall be fine," said Alice.

"The race is all the crew are talking about," said Charlie, as they hurried on.

"Yes, I saw it mentioned in a newspaper Dorothy was reading. How does the race work exactly?" asked Sonny.

"When a ship crosses the Atlantic the time is recorded after it passes Bishop Rock Lighthouse, just off the Isles of Scilly, and then again at the Lightship *Ambrose* which marks the entrance to New York Harbour's shipping channel," said Charlie, grabbing the rope rail as the ship listed. "The ship passing between the two points in the quickest time wins the trophy. If we win, it will mean more passengers, freight contracts and more tips for us," he said with a look of glee.

"If the ship wins, my father may also get promoted, which means we'll get to spend more time together. He's obsessed with the race though, so I don't see much of him now," Alice said to Charlie, unable to hide the disappointment in her voice.

"That sounds a little like me and Dorothy," said Sonny, wrinkling his nose.

"She's still acting strangely then?" asked Charlie, smiling at an elderly couple coming out of their cabin.

Sonny gave a reluctant nod. The ship rolled and he grabbed Charlie's arm to steady himself. "Dorothy is normally strict about me keeping up with school lessons through the summer, but this year she's letting me come and go as I please."

"Do you see your parents over the summer?" asked Alice, thinking how fun it would be to arrive somewhere new each day, rather than spending hours in the same classroom with the same boring view of the school playing field.

"Dorothy is my governess and guardian. I don't have any family," said Sonny matter-of-factly.

"Oh. I'm sorry," said Alice, worrying she might have upset him. She had occasionally been hurt by careless questions about her own mother, but Sonny waved a hand, indicating he wasn't offended.

"Dorothy insists we do schoolwork in the ship's library and it's deathly quiet and dull in there. I try and make friends if I see any passengers around my own age, but they always go home after a few days. I sometimes wonder what that feels like – to have a home to go to, I mean," continued

Sonny. He looked wistful and Alice gave him a sympathetic look as they passed a glass wall case displaying ties and handkerchiefs for sale in one of the ship's shops. Even though she missed her father and aunt, there was always someone to talk to and share a joke with at her school. She could see how his life might get lonely.

"If you don't mind me asking, why do you and Dorothy live at sea? I can't imagine what it must be like to be on a ship for all those months," said Alice.

"It is unusual, but my grandfather loved the sea. He thought I'd have a better education travelling, than by living in one place," said Sonny. "Dorothy makes sure we move to a different ship every once in a while, but a couple of months after my grandfather died we boarded the *Queen Mary* and we've been here ever since."

"At least you've had time to make friends with some of the crew while having your swimming lessons," said Charlie with a twinkle in his eye.

"Yes. Although I think you lot thought I was stuck up to begin with, travelling in first class," said Sonny with a grimace, as if embarrassed at his privilege.

"That's true," said Charlie with a grin. "But it turns out you were different from those other toffs who act like we're invisible."

Alice smiled, feeling pleased that Sonny had some friends on board.

"Anyway, I'm glad *I* don't have to go to school any more," said Charlie, making a face as he strode along.

"You didn't enjoy it then?" asked Alice, hurrying to keep up and thinking what different lives the three of them had.

Charlie shook his head. "Letters and numbers never made much sense to me. I joined Cunard, the shipping company that owns the *Queen Mary*, last year when I was fourteen, just like my older brother did. Except he works on a different ship as a luggage handler, so I don't see him as much as I'd like."

Charlie's mention of his brother's job made Alice think of the keys to her mother's luggage. "There's something I'd like to see in the ship's hold. Do you know how I might get in there?" she said. The floor beneath her feet rose and fell and her stomach swooped.

"I'm afraid the hold is closed to passengers," said Sonny.

Charlie smirked. "You could ask your father. He spends enough time down there when we're in port – it's become a bit of a mystery."

"What does he do down there?" asked Alice, keen to learn more.

"Maybe I've spoken out of turn," said Charlie, giving Alice an anxious glance.

"No, go on," said Alice, as they held back and waited for a couple with wind-blown hair and rosy cheeks to walk past.

"When we dock in New York and the baggage has been unloaded, your father sends the luggage handlers off to get a drink. He uses that time to visit the forward hold alone. The rumour is he inspects the ropes and pulleys, which is odd as that isn't his responsibility. No one knows for sure what he does down there."

Alice bit the inside of her cheek. Could her father be down there looking at her mother's luggage? But why the secrecy? She thought again of the detective bureau card. It seemed there was a lot more she didn't know about her father.

Charlie ground to a halt, his face suddenly anxious as voices came from down the corridor. "There's the head liftman talking to one of the other bellboys. We need to go a different way," he said, swivelling and leading them quickly back the way they'd come. Turning a corner in the passageway they were met with a closed door marked *Third-Class passenger area.* Taking a bunch of keys from his pocket, Charlie selected one and unlocked the door.

"Are we allowed in there?" asked Alice, looking back to see if Charlie's supervisor had followed them. She felt a fresh concern at being caught.

"First-class passengers, like Sonny, are free to wander wherever they like. They just need to ask a member of the crew to let them through the locked doors to second and third-class areas. It doesn't work the other way around though," Charlie replied simply.

"But that's hardly fair," said Alice with a frown, as the three of them slipped through the door and Charlie locked it behind them.

"Money opens doors," said Charlie with a shrug.

Sonny's cheeks pinked and Alice sensed again he was a little embarrassed by his own position. His grandfather must have been extraordinarily wealthy to allow him and his guardian to live at sea like this.

"Come on," urged Charlie. "We need to get through here as quickly as we can."

Alice saw the lush carpets of the upper decks were replaced here by a linoleum floor. But the biggest difference was that instead of the quietness of the upper decks, cabin doors had been propped open and there was the sound of laughter.

"Hello," said a young woman with a smile as they

walked past, gently rocking a sleeping baby in her arms.

"Good evening," nodded a man who was preparing to play a silver flute as two small children looked on. As he began a lively tune the children clapped their hands in delight.

"If I had all the money in the world, I'd rather pay for a cabin down here than upstairs," said Charlie, doffing his cap to an older gentleman who was sitting in his cabin doorway and tapping his feet in time to the music.

"Yes. I can see why," agreed Alice, enjoying the area's warm glow of friendship and family.

Charlie led them through another locked door and Alice saw they were now close to the first-class stairwell she had used when visiting the pool that morning. It was a stark contrast to the area they had just left; a muted hum of conversation came from men in dinner suits and women in gowns of emerald satin and delicate navy crêpe as they headed to the upper decks for pre-dinner drinks.

Alice kept her head down, anxious to remain inconspicuous as they hurried along, but they were not given a second glance as they quietly slipped through the swimming-pool doors.

A thin-faced woman wearing a swimming cap was ploughing steadily up and down the pool, as water sloshed in time with the ship's movement. The memory of Joseph's fall echoed in Alice's head as she quietly followed Sonny and Charlie to the balcony steps. The swimmer would have no clue there had been a terrible accident earlier in the day. She turned her head mid-stroke and gave them all a curious glance. She began to tread water and Alice noticed her expression had slipped into a frown.

Reaching the top of the steps, Alice looked along the dimly lit walkway in front of the nine changing cubicles. She felt growing excitement as she began searching out where Joseph might have hidden the package. There were no gaps or crevices in the tiles which might suggest a hiding place. She turned to the cubicles. "It could be hidden in one of those," she whispered, gesturing to the wooden enclosures.

"You and Sonny start in the end cubicles, and I'll start in the middle," suggested Charlie.

Giving a nod of acknowledgement, Alice began her search. The cubicle was open at both the floor and ceiling. That really left one potential hiding place and that was under the bench seat. Crouching, she ran her fingers beneath the varnished wood but found nothing.

Exiting the small space, Alice threw a quick look over the balcony. To her surprise she saw the pool was empty.

The woman who had been swimming had left. She leaned over further and saw her standing by the door in her robe. She was glaring directly at Alice. The crash of water breaking over the side of the pool as the ship rocked bounced an eerie echo off the wall tiles.

Feeling anxious, Alice ducked down behind the balcony. Sonny and Charlie emerged empty-handed from the cubicles they had been searching and she gestured for them to get down too. They did so quickly, throwing her questioning looks. "The woman in the pool. She's watching us," she hissed.

Charlie cautiously peeped over the balcony. "But... there's no one there," he said.

A sliver of cold danced across Alice's shoulders. She saw he was right. There was no sign of the woman, but she hadn't heard anyone leave. "We need to finish looking and get out of here," she whispered.

As the ship creaked, Alice headed into another cubicle and once more felt under the bench. Nothing. Sighing with frustration, she moved to the final enclosure and repeated her search. This time her fingers grazed over something lumpy wedged into the gap between the underside of the bench and the wall. Her heart gave an extra-hard thump. "Come in here. I've found something," she said in a low voice.

Sonny and Charlie poked their heads round the door, watching intently as Alice prised it free and held it up. It was small, about the width of two hands. "It's heavy," she whispered, passing it to Sonny.

Sonny drew in a breath as he felt the package's weight.

Charlie pointed to the brown wrapping paper. "The letter R's been handwritten on the front. What does that mean?"

Sonny frowned. "Do we open it?"

Alice thought about the swimming woman and the inquisitive look in her eyes. "No. Not here."

"How about your cabin then?" Charlie suggested to Sonny.

"As long as we're done before Dorothy returns from her pre-dinner drink," said Sonny with a nod, slipping the package under his jumper.

Leaving the pool, Alice hurried up the stairs with Sonny and Charlie, but a feeling made her glance back. Standing outside the pool entrance and speaking on the telephone was the woman who had been swimming. Her elongated face was pulled into a strangely furious look as she spoke in a hushed tone to the person on the other end of the line. Feeling a jolt of unease, Alice lowered her head and hurried on.

Chapter 11

PACKAGE

Alice's uneasy thoughts about the woman from the swimming pool were pushed to one side as she took in Sonny's cabin on Main Deck. Her sandals sank into the peach carpet of the living area. The sofa and easy chair, table with a large vase of fragrant blooms and electric fireplace made it appear more like a fancy apartment than a cabin. The articles stuck in her adventures scrapbook said suites like this one were among the most expensive at sea, reserved for only the wealthiest guests. And to think Sonny had been living like this for months on end!

Sonny placed the package they had found on the table

beside a pretty wooden keepsake box.

"Go on then, open it," instructed Charlie, stepping over and folding his arms.

"You think we should?" asked Sonny uncertainly.

"I'll do it," said Charlie, tutting in mock annoyance. He picked the package up and unsealed it. Reaching inside, he pulled out an item about the size of his palm that made Sonny draw in a breath of surprise.

"A gold ingot!" Alice exclaimed.

Charlie placed the packaging on the table and turned the oblong of gleaming gold over in his hands. "Jeepers. I've never seen anything like this. Imagine what it's worth!" he said.

"May I see?" asked Sonny, letting out a low whistle as he examined the gold under an arrow of sunlight from a porthole.

Alice bent down and slipped a hand inside the empty packaging. "There's something else," she said, pulling out a piece of paper. Unfolding it, she saw it was written on *Queen Mary* headed notepaper; the type she knew was found in every passenger cabin on board.

Second payment will be handed over after job is complete.

"What the heck does that mean?" said Charlie with a frown, leaning over to see.

"This gold is payment for something," said Sonny darkly. "Could R be a person do you think?"

"I reckon so," said Charlie, examining the initial printed on the front of the package. "But I don't think this package can be for Joseph – there are no Rs in his name."

"I wonder who it's for then?" said Alice.

"It must be for someone on board as there's no address," said Sonny.

Charlie looked thoughtful. "A passenger could easily pass something like this to a fellow passenger, but it might be more difficult to deliver a package to a member of the ship's crew."

Sonny turned to Alice. "You overheard the man who pushed Joseph say something about the Pig and Whistle. That could be a clue."

"The crew pub?" said Charlie in surprise.

Alice pressed a hand to her forehead as she tried to recall exactly what she had overheard. "I think the man said, 'What about the Pig and Whistle?' and it was after that Joseph said he'd changed his mind about taking it."

"Changed his mind about taking it," mused Sonny. "Changed his mind about passing on the package to someone in the pub perhaps?"

"Yes," said Charlie excitedly. "Joseph could have been

intending to give this package to a member of the ship's crew in the Pig and Whistle. It could be for someone who doesn't mingle with passengers; like a chef in the kitchens perhaps, or a stoker in the boiler room."

"I suppose that would explain why Joseph's help was needed in passing the package on," said Alice, glancing again at the note and wondering what the job was.

"Do you have any idea who this R might be?" Sonny asked Charlie hopefully.

Charlie wrinkled his nose. "There are over one thousand crew on board this ship, and most visit the Pig and Whistle from time to time. There are Ritas, Roberts, Richards... some Ralphs and Ruths. Then there are the surnames beginning with R..." He paused and shook his head. "There are too many. I can't think how we'd narrow it down."

"Oh," said Alice, seeing this was a problem. "Well at least we can assume Joseph was planning on showing you the ingot and the note at the pool," she said to Sonny, pleased they had an explanation for why Joseph had asked to meet him there.

"I wouldn't have been late to meet Joseph if it hadn't been for..." began Sonny. He paused and flicked his eyes to a closed door to their right, then pressed his lips together.

Alice looked at the door, briefly wondering what had held him up that morning.

Charlie took the gold from Sonny and ran his fingers over its smooth surface. "My brother said crew members were sometimes approached by passengers to smuggle alcohol into America when it was banned up until a couple of years ago. They were paid well for the risk, sometimes in gold like this. Bottles of whiskey were once hidden in empty coffins on a ship my brother worked on. This ingot could be payment to a crew member for something illegal like that."

"Goodness," said Alice, not liking the thought at all. This was suddenly rather serious and a reality she hadn't considered when yearning for an adventure. "Do you think Joseph might have been involved in something like that?"

"Not knowingly," said Charlie, shaking his head vehemently. "Joseph found the staff captain's dropped wallet once and handed it in. He's very honourable."

Alice nodded, feeling pleased Joseph had helped her father in that way. She thought back again to the argument. "Joseph told the man who pushed him that he'd expose what he was doing. That meant Joseph must have known what was inside the package and maybe what it was for." Stepping over to the porthole, she looked out at the white-capped swells as she tried to piece together how Joseph might have become entangled with the passenger. "The accident record said Joseph is steward to cabins A80–99. Does he work in those cabins on every voyage?" she asked, turning to face the boys.

Charlie frowned. "I think so. Why?"

"Would he speak with his passengers much?" asked Alice, thinking of Pearl and her delivery of meals, fresh towels and friendly conversation.

"Certainly. Stewards work from seven o'clock in the morning until ten o'clock in the evening with only a short afternoon break. They're always cleaning cabins and making sure their passengers are well cared for," said Charlie with a nod.

"So that might explain how Joseph and this passenger got to know one other," mused Alice.

"That does seem logical," said Sonny.

"I think I know where you're going with this," said Charlie. "The incident at the pool happened on the second morning of the voyage, but there was more than a day's history between Joseph and the person who pushed him."

"Of course. So this passenger, the person who pushed him, has travelled on this ship before and most likely in one of the cabins Joseph serviced," said Sonny, puffing out a small breath at this realization.

"Yes," said Alice excitedly. "If we can find out who stayed in cabins A80–99 over the last few crossings, I think we'll find someone who has taken repeat voyages."

"And the man who pushed Joseph," said Charlie with a grimace.

"Gosh," said Sonny, his face brightening. "Are you sure you haven't done any detective work before, Alice?"

Alice grinned. She wasn't a fan of puzzle books or mathematics, but thinking things through together in the hope they could solve this mystery was proving to be very satisfying.

"We should hide the gold and the note for now," said Charlie, slipping both items back into the package and sealing it as best he could. He turned to Sonny. "How about in your room under your mattress?"

Sonny's face dropped into a frown as he glanced at the same door he'd looked at before. He chewed on his lower lip.

Charlie smiled. "You can't keep him a secret for ever, Sonny. I reckon you can trust Alice."

"Him?" repeated Alice, looking at them both quizzically. "What on earth are you talking about?"

Sonny groaned. "But Alice's father is the staff captain. What will he say if he finds out?"

Throwing Sonny a confused look, Alice strode to the door, more curious than ever.

"No...wait!" called Sonny, but Alice ignored him, flung open the door and stared at the unexpected sight before her.

Chapter 12

ROCKET

Alice stepped into Sonny's cabin and peered at the small wire cage on his bedside table. Inside, a pocket-sized silvery mouse scuffled around amid a pile of shredded newspaper and wood shavings.

"This is Rocket," said Sonny, following Alice. Opening the cage door, he carefully took out the mouse, who sniffed his tiny pink nose, scampered up Sonny's right arm and round his shirt collar. "You're not afraid of mice, are you?" he asked anxiously.

"Of course not," huffed Alice, offended he'd even thought to ask that question.

"Please don't tell your father. He'll have him taken away," said Sonny worriedly, as Rocket snuffled his ear.

"Of course I won't tell. But how have you managed to keep him a secret? Pets aren't allowed in cabins," said Alice.

"Our steward knows about him, but he's promised to keep quiet. Rocket was my grandfather's mouse. He bred them, you see. Most were rehomed after he died, but Rocket was a pup then – that's the name for a baby mouse – and my favourite. I couldn't let him go, so I smuggled him on board."

"What did Dorothy think about that?" asked Alice.

"She was very cross, but I begged her to let him stay. She agreed in the end," said Sonny. "The only problem is his cage is small and he often fusses until I come and get him out. That's what happened the day I was late to meet Joseph." He gave Alice a sidelong look. "Would you like to hold him?"

Rocket had coal-black eyes, long fine whiskers and his shiny coat reminded Alice of the moon on a clear night. He really was rather sweet. She nodded and Sonny carefully placed him in Alice's cupped palms. His feet tickled her skin and she smiled. "I must say this is a surprise. A nice one though."

"Don't you mean a *mice* one," said Charlie with a grin.

Alice rolled her eyes and Sonny laughed.

As Rocket lived up to his name and raced up Alice's arm, she noticed a few photographs on Sonny's bedside table next to a pair of binoculars and a jar of seeds and grains, which she presumed to be mouse food. A fair-haired woman, perhaps a similar age to her father, with a delicate nose and kind-looking eyes, held a young boy's hand, while the impressive Golden Gate Bridge in San Francisco soared behind them. The boy was curling into the woman's side shyly, as if trying to hide behind her skirts and the woman was looking at him adoringly. "Is that you and Dorothy?" she asked.

"Yes. Grandfather took that picture," said Sonny, pointing to another photograph of an elderly man with slicked-back hair sitting in a wicker rocking chair, Sonny standing to one side looking sombre in a dark suit.

"Photography is Dorothy's hobby, although she hasn't done much of it since we've been on board the *Queen Mary*," said Sonny with a frown, lifting one end of his bunk mattress and carefully hiding the package Charlie had passed to him.

The other photographs showed Sonny framed by palm trees, pearly white beaches, magnificent buildings with cascading towers and ancient ruins. Alice felt a jolt of envy;

he would have been able to fill her adventures scrapbook ten times over with everything he'd seen and done.

"How long has Dorothy looked after you?" asked Alice, as Sonny carefully plucked Rocket from Alice's shoulder and passed him to Charlie.

"My parents died in a motor-car accident about twelve years ago," Sonny replied as he watched Rocket sniff the brass buttons on Charlie's jacket, perhaps hoping they were something tasty to nibble on. "I don't remember them. I was only two when it happened, so Grandfather employed a nanny from London. Dorothy arrived and has been with me ever since." He took a deep breath, his cheeks pinking. "We often stayed with my grandfather between voyages. I liked it. I sometimes wish Dorothy and I could have a proper home, a garden, and some animals." He threw an affectionate look at Rocket.

"Doesn't Dorothy have family of her own?" asked Alice, thinking it was a bit peculiar that the two of them had been on the *Queen Mary* for so long. Even she could see that might get boring after a while.

Sonny shook his head and looked up. "She was orphaned when she was young, like me. Dorothy and I have always been close, she's like a mother really. But for some reason that's changed since we've been on board this ship." He paused and Alice sensed he had more to say but needed to build up the courage to say it.

"I worry Dorothy regrets taking me on," Sonny continued slowly. "I think we're steaming east and west across the Atlantic because she can't decide what to do with me now Grandfather's died."

"I'm sure that's not the case," said Charlie softly, passing Sonny his mouse.

"My mother died when I was a baby too," said Alice, her throat suddenly tight. "My aunt cared for me while my father was away at sea, and I know she loves me. I'm sure Dorothy wants to be with you too."

Sonny gave Alice a sorry smile. "I'm sorry about your mother."

"Me too," said Charlie quietly.

They sat in silence for a few moments and Alice was surprised to find it soothing rather than awkward.

"Enough of my worries," said Sonny eventually, returning Rocket to his cage. He stood up. "We need to think about helping Joseph."

"What do we do next? I don't like the thought that someone is up to no good on this ship," said Charlie.

"My father has a passenger list for this voyage on his desk. I could try and find the previous lists to identify who stayed in the cabins Joseph worked in. Anyone who travelled in them more than once that might be the passenger we're looking for," said Alice.

Sonny nodded in approval and glanced at Charlie. "Perhaps you could think some more about the crew and who this R might be," he suggested. He glanced at his watch. "Dorothy will be back soon. We'd better leave this for now."

Saying goodbye to her new friends, Alice arranged to meet them the following morning. Hurrying back to her cabin, she kept to hushed corridors and quiet stairwells, all the while keeping a sharp eye out for Mrs Cuthbert and any sign of her father.

As she walked, Alice thought of everything they knew: Joseph had got mixed up with a passenger, a crime had been committed and he'd been deliberately hurt. Joseph had hidden a package and intended to show it to Sonny, and that package contained gold as payment for what was likely to be an underhand job, possibly being undertaken by a member of the ship's crew known only as R. There was so much they needed to investigate, and it was already Friday evening. In a little over two days, the person who hurt Joseph would disembark from the ship in New York and get away with their bad deeds. Alice gritted her teeth; they could not allow that to happen.

Chapter 13

PASSENGER MANIFEST

"**O**ld passenger manifests," said Pearl, placing two clean towels on the end of Alice's bed later that evening. "What would you be wanting with those?" She glanced at the adventures scrapbook lying on the bunk that Alice had been busy updating with the afternoon's events.

Alice's cheeks felt hot, and she closed the book and placed her pencil on top of it. The motion of the ship caused the pencil to roll onto the floor and she bent to retrieve it. She couldn't tell Pearl the truth, for then her father might get to hear of it, but she hated lying too. She had carefully searched her father's cabin for the passenger lists from previous voyages, but they were nowhere to be found. She needed help and Pearl seemed the logical choice. "One of my friends was on board the ship...a few weeks ago. I was curious to see...which cabin she travelled in," she said haltingly, glancing up at Pearl.

"Is that right?" said Pearl, folding her arms. She didn't seem for one minute to have been fooled by Alice's lie.

Alice fiddled with the pencil, her flush deepening.

"Passenger manifests are kept up here in the room for officers' stewards. I suppose there isn't any harm in you looking at them," said Pearl.

Alice threw Pearl a grateful smile.

The stewards' room was small and windowless, containing a shelf of neatly stacked clean uniforms, a seating area and a hostess trolley for delivering meals to the officers' cabins.

On the far wall was a cupboard and Pearl strode over to it. "Here you are," she said, pointing out a stack of cardboard magazine files resting beside some key hooks. "Passenger manifests for the last few months are kept on board, in case there's an issue with lost property. You'd be amazed how often people leave something behind. Last week a gold pocket watch was found under a bed. How do you forget something like that?"

Passing a wadge of manifests to Alice, Pearl accidentally jostled a key from its hook and it fell to the floor.

Alice picked it up and returned it to the hook, noticing the typed card above it. *Cabin Master Key.*

Pearl grimaced. "Thank you. Officers are worse at mislaying their cabin keys than passengers. Pays to keep one of these close to hand."

They walked back along the passageway towards Alice's cabin, swaying as the ship lurched. "I'm pleased your father invited you on board, Alice. He's been happier since you've been here and that's nice to see," Pearl said.

"Really?" asked Alice, feeling glad that was the case.

"Yes. It's important families are together. So many were separated when the *Titanic* went down. It certainly made me appreciate spending time with my own family," said Pearl.

Alice gave Pearl a shy glance. "Can you tell me what it was like on the *Titanic*? Father's only told me a little, but he wasn't there."

Pearl's forehead wrinkled. "It was quite desperate. You must already know there weren't enough lifeboats on board for all the passengers. Women and children were given priority and I was bustled into a boat which was only half full. It was very dark by that point and a stewardess next to me, Violet Jessop was her name, was handed a baby by an officer. No one knew where the poor mite's parents were."

"That must have been so frightening," said Alice, finding it hard to imagine the terror everyone had felt.

"It was. I remember feeling so heartbroken for the poor babe as we swaddled it in blankets. It was a long, cold night. I had a packet of lemon sherbets in my pocket and shared them round. They made me think of home – and feel braver somehow. Then another ship, the *Carpathia* arrived to rescue us. Do you know, the baby's mother had already been rescued and was aboard that ship? She whisked the child from Violet's arms without so much as a thank you, or a kind word, and we never saw her again."

"Poor Violet," said Alice, images of that terrifying night on the open ocean making her feel quite cold.

"It didn't put Violet off working at sea. She survived the sinking of the *Britannic* during the Great War too and has even been named 'Miss Unsinkable' by some." Pearl paused and looked at Alice. "Be careful, won't you, Alice."

"I'm not sure what you mean," Alice said, her grip tightening on the passenger manifests.

"Your father's told me about instructing you to stay on the upper decks. But I saw you on D Deck talking with

Charlie and another boy earlier today," Pearl said, her eyes narrowing.

"Oh," said Alice, her shoulders sagging. She hadn't seen Pearl, which proved how easy it was to be spotted, and how careless she'd been.

"I don't agree with your father, but I don't want you to get into hot water either," Pearl whispered.

Alice chewed on her bottom lip. "Please don't tell him. He's so busy with the race and it's just...I've made some friends and I so wanted to explore the ship."

"Befriending a bellboy is a little unusual," Pearl said quizzically.

Pearl had been kind and Alice saw she owed her a small portion of the truth. "Charlie's helping us. We have...a mystery that needs solving," she said.

"A mystery at sea! How intriguing," said Pearl. With an indulgent smile, she reached into her apron pocket and pulled out a small paper packet. "Here, take these. Maybe they will bring you some luck with solving your mystery. They certainly helped me on the *Titanic*."

Alice peered into the packet to see a few sugar-coated lemon sherbets. "Thank you," she said, feeling touched by the gesture as she stuffed them into a pocket in her slacks.

The following morning Alice sipped her orange juice while breakfasting with her father, all the while thinking of the passenger manifests. She'd pored over them late into the evening, searching for anyone who'd been a frequent passenger in Joseph's cabins, until her eyes had grown heavy and the light from the porthole had faded. She slipped a hand in her dress pocket and felt for the tip of the folded paper containing the information she had discovered. Her hand curled into a fist in anticipation of telling Charlie and Sonny all she had found out.

"What do you plan to do today?" her father asked, finishing his slice of toast and cherry jam.

"Um... Maybe a stroll around Sun Deck, and then some embroidery," said Alice, hoping her father didn't detect the lie.

"Jolly good. Take a cardigan though, fog is forecast this afternoon," her father said with a frown. "The captain will want to reduce the ship to half speed, and I shall have to try and persuade him otherwise. It's Saturday and we arrive in New York in two days. We must push on if we are to achieve another 750 nautical miles by midday and the same again tomorrow."

Alice felt a ripple of unease at the looming weather – and how little time they had to solve the mystery of who had hurt Joseph. "You've always said fog at sea is dangerous."

Her father shook his head. "The ship is on a course to cross the Atlantic in a record-breaking time. We can't let some fog affect that. There are many rivals out there who would dearly love us to lose the race, like the current holder of the trophy, the *Sapphire*. We can't have that, can we?"

"I suppose not," said Alice, her mind turning to the *Titanic* and her conversation with Pearl the day before. That ship had been travelling too swiftly in an area prone to icebergs. Some people said this was because it had been trying to cross the Atlantic in a faster time than its sister ship, the *Olympic*. Speed and safety didn't always sit comfortably together, whatever the stakes.

"There's nothing to worry about," her father said, pushing back his chair, standing up and putting on his hat. "No disaster will befall this ship. Not while I'm second in command."

Alice gave him an uncertain smile, dearly hoping he was right, but even as she thought this, her mind flickered back to Joseph. A disaster had already befallen this ship – if only her father knew.

Chapter 14

MIRIAM

"Good morning, would you care to step inside my office?" said Charlie, doffing his hat to Alice as she and Sonny arrived at the stern passenger lifts a little after nine o'clock.

Alice grinned. Charlie was one of the sunniest people she had ever met, always with an easy smile and a joke to hand. As she stepped inside the lift, she saw it would be a safe and private space, away from prying eyes and ears, as they talked.

"Have you any news on Joseph?" asked Sonny, as the lift doors closed.

"Yes, and it's not good," said Charlie, his smile quickly fading. "I stopped by the hospital and Joseph still hasn't woken. That's not good after a head injury." He pressed a button and the lift glided upwards, its varnished wooden walls giving off the pleasant aroma of polish. "I also had a look at the crew manifest last night," he continued. "There are thirty-six crew with names beginning with the letter R. I'd say that's too many to investigate in the two days we have left."

"I might have had some better luck," said Alice, pulling from her dress pocket the paper containing the information she had gleaned from the passenger manifests.

<u>People who have travelled in cabins A80–99</u>
<u>more than once and are currently on board</u>

<u>Mr and Mrs F. Blake</u>
Travelled four times on the Queen Mary in the last month.
Stayed in cabin A96 each time.

<u>Mr and Mrs K. Fraser</u>
Travelled six times on the Queen Mary over last two-and-a-half months.
Stayed in cabins A80 and A85 and currently in cabin A98.

"It's going to be difficult to work out who this R is, but at least we have some passengers to investigate. Well done," said Charlie, causing Alice's cheeks to flush with pleasure.

Sonny looked thoughtful. "What now?"

"We need to observe these passengers," said Alice firmly, having already decided this was the most sensible thing to do. "If I can hear Mr Blake and Mr Fraser speak, I might recognize one of them as the man who hurt Joseph. I'll never forget his voice."

"But what if they get suspicious?" asked Sonny, his worry lines deepening. He leaned back against the wall. "We can't risk them finding out what we are doing."

Alice understood Sonny's anxiety, but they had a plan now and she was glad of that. Putting names to the passengers who had potentially hurt Joseph brought what they were trying to do into sharper focus. "I'm a bit afraid too, but we can't let that stop us, especially as Joseph hasn't woken up."

"She's right," said Charlie, pressing another button on the control panel and frowning at a smudge on the lift wall. "We need to find out who did this before the ship docks in New York and the culprit scarpers." He pulled a cloth from his pocket and quickly polished the smudge away.

The lift shuddered to a stop and the doors opened. The children looked at each other silently, each absorbing the terrible thought.

"We're on A Deck now," said Charlie, peeping out of the lift.

Sonny gave a wan smile. "And I suppose that's a coincidence?"

Charlie shrugged. "Just doing my bit to help with the investigation."

"Thank you, Charlie," said Sonny, shaking his head. "Alice and I can loiter along the passageway close to cabins A96 and A98 and follow whoever comes out first. We need to keep well back though and make sure we're not seen. We also need to stick together."

Alice threw Charlie a quick smile. "We'll be sure to let you know what we find. I'll keep notes," she said pulling a pencil from her pocket. "I can write everything up later."

Sonny gave her an amused glance. "Like a proper detective?"

Alice shrugged. "I have this book. I call it my adventures scrapbook...except...well...this is the first adventure of my own I can write about. And I suppose this is more of a mystery really...but still..." She paused, feeling suddenly flustered.

"I think that's a jolly sensible idea," said Sonny seriously. "A good detective always makes notes."

Halfway along the passageway, Alice paused. "Do you hear that?" she whispered.

Sonny nodded. A low rhythmic *thud, thud, thud* could be heard a short way ahead.

They hurried on, the sound becoming louder by the second. "What do you think it is?" asked Alice.

"I don't know. But it seems to be coming from in there," Sonny replied, pointing to one of the narrow corridors which allowed people to move between the port and starboard sides of the ship.

Alice and Sonny peered down the gap to see a girl with dark bobbed hair kicking the heels of her brown sandals against a wall. Her kicks were fierce, matching the expression on her face.

The girl looked up when she saw Alice and Sonny watching. Her cheeks were flushed, her gaze bristling.

Alice saw they must be about the same age, and she wondered what had caused the girl to be so cross. She glanced at Sonny, and he shrugged.

"Um...hello. Is everything...all right?" Alice asked the

girl curiously, stepping forward.

The girl stared at Alice. Her forehead scrunched into a frown, as if she was searching for exactly the right words. "I bumped into a man. He shouted at me," she said, with a German accent. Her eyes narrowed. "I said sorry but still he shouted."

"How rotten," said Sonny.

"I do not get cross at such small things," the girl continued fiercely, as if disappointed at herself. "But Mami and Papi stay in our cabin all day, except when we go out to eat. I worry about that too."

"Oh dear. Are your parents unwell?" asked Sonny, looking concerned.

"No. It is because we have left Germany. We left everything. Even my goldfish," she said with a heavy sigh.

Alice felt a burst of dismay. "But why did you have to leave everything behind?"

The girl's eyes darkened. There was a *thud* as she kicked the wall again. "We left quickly. It was not safe. *Der Führer* – Adolf Hitler – does not want Jewish families like ours in Germany. We are going to America to live with my *onkel* in California. Papi spent all our money on permits and tickets. Now he and Mami are busy and have many forms to fill in and letters to write as they plan our new life."

"Is that why they stay inside your cabin?" asked Sonny.

The girl nodded. "Mami and Papi tell me to go and explore the ship but I find this hard. I cannot stop thinking about...everything."

The way the girl said "everything" made Alice suspect this included some not very nice things, and her heart squeezed. The girl had left her country and family behind, her home and possessions too. A new science teacher at school, Mr Holzer, had recently arrived from Germany and had told Alice's class of his struggle to obtain a visa to allow him to live and work in Britain. He'd told the class that the new Nazi state was deciding what jobs Jewish people could do and who they could marry. As a result some people were trying to flee the country in search of a new and better life. Alice did not understand why anyone would impose rules that affected people this way.

Alice looked at the girl now, strongly feeling that, in her position, she would not want to be alone. She wished there was something she could do to help and then she saw, in a small way, that she could. "I'm Alice and this is Sonny," she said. "Perhaps we could be friends while you're on board?"

"Jolly good idea. It might help take your mind off things," said Sonny.

The girl's face lit up with a sudden grin. "I am Miriam

Brunn and I would like that." Miriam's stomach gurgled. She folded her arms round the waistband of her blue cotton skirt and gave them an apologetic look.

"Oh. Have you not eaten breakfast?" asked Alice.

Miriam shook her head. "Mami and Papi worked long into the night on their letters and forms. We woke late."

"Well, we must sort that at once," said Sonny brightly, gesturing for Miriam and Alice to follow him. "Your steward will be able to deliver breakfast to the cabin if that's easier? I can show you how to arrange that later if you like?"

Miriam gave him a grateful nod and they all set off along the passageway.

"We should hurry before the man who shouted returns," Miriam said, gesturing at a cabin door as they walked past.

Alice followed Miriam's pointed finger and stared in surprise at the brass plate on the door. *Cabin A98.*

Sonny puffed out a small breath. "The Frasers' cabin," he whispered.

Alice nodded. The very people they needed to find. "You're certain it was the man from that cabin you bumped into?" she asked Miriam.

"Yes. You know this man?" asked Miriam, her eyes widening in alarm.

"Um no, we don't," said Sonny, raising his eyebrows at Alice.

Alice threw a last lingering look at Cabin A98 as they hurried along the passageway. It sounded as if Mr Fraser had been awful to Miriam when she bumped into him. Was that a sign he was the person who had hurt Joseph too?

Sonny led them to the Garden Lounge on Promenade Deck. Feeling a niggle of worry at being spotted by her father or Pearl, Alice selected a table behind a large hydrangea with fragrant pink blooms that seemed out of place against the rolling waves outside the window.

A waitress approached. "May I fetch you tea and pastries?"

"Yes please," said Sonny. "Some of those chocolate fondants with vanilla icing would be nice. Oh, and some apple turnovers too, if you have them."

The waitress nodded and quickly returned with a stand laden with an impressive assortment of miniature cakes and glazed pastries. She proceeded to serve them tea in china cups.

Miriam chewed on her bottom lip. "Our meals in the restaurant are included in our fare, but I have no money for this," she said in a low voice. "Papi used all his savings on this voyage. Only first-class tickets were left."

"Don't worry," said Alice with a smile. "The cakes here are included too."

Sonny grinned. "You can eat as many as you like and, believe me, plenty of people do."

A slow smile stole onto Miriam's cheeks too, and she selected a chocolate fondant and sank her teeth into it. She let out a small groan of pleasure. "Mami would like this very much. Papi would bring us cakes from the corner bakery on his way home from work." Her expression changed, like a dark cloud slipping across the sun. "The bakery has closed. The owners were upset at the new laws and left Germany, like us. I heard them tell Papi they were afraid war is coming."

Alice exchanged an uneasy glance with Sonny, as she remembered the headlines in the daily newspapers delivered to school. She and her friend Gloria sometimes sneaked one from the top of the pile to scan the cinema listings, and it was impossible to avoid news of the growing conflict in Europe. The British government was insisting war could be avoided, but just a few days ago a civil war had broken out in Spain. The thought of all this unrest made Alice's stomach tumble with anxiety, especially as her grandfather on her father's side had fought in the Great War and lost his life. She wanted to say something comforting, but couldn't think what could possibly help Miriam feel better.

"Please...can I ask a question?" said Miriam, taking another bite of her cake and looking at them through slightly narrowed eyes.

Alice pushed the uncomfortable thoughts away and nodded.

"When I pointed to the cabin of the man who shouted at me you looked surprised. Why?" continued Miriam.

Alice and Sonny exchanged a glance. "We should tell her," suggested Sonny.

"Yes, I think we should. She's our friend and she may be able to help," said Alice.

Sonny leaned forward and quickly told Miriam they were searching for the occupants of cabins A96 and A98.

"One of Sonny's friends – a steward – is hurt. These people might have had something to do with it, but I need to hear their voices to be certain," said Alice under her breath, before taking a bite of an apple turnover.

Miriam selected a pastry and placed it in on her plate. She frowned. "I am sorry about your friend."

"Did you notice anything unusual about the Frasers?

Before Mr Fraser shouted at you, I mean," asked Alice.

"I bumped into his big bag. That is why he shouted," Miriam said, shaking her fist to indicate just how cross Mr Fraser had been.

"That's curious. I wonder what's inside it?" Sonny pondered, licking vanilla icing from his fingers.

Alice thought of the note and the second payment promised to R after the job was complete. Could a second gold ingot be hidden in the Frasers' cabin?

"Excuse me," said a voice.

Alice looked up to see a man in a dark suit and tie holding a cloth and a small brass watering can.

"Do you mind if I lean over and polish the leaves of the plants. The salt water gets to them you see," he explained.

"Of course," said Alice, moving her chair.

"Could you help us identify the Frasers, Miriam? If Alice can hear Mr Fraser speaking, that might tell us who hurt my friend," whispered Sonny, throwing an anxious glance at the man, but he was absorbed in polishing the plant's dark leaves to a high gloss and did not seem to be listening to their conversation.

Miriam gave a decisive nod. "They were leaving their cabin when I bumped into them. Mrs Fraser wore a scarf. Blue and red. And they had a blanket."

"Maybe they went to sit out on deck?" Sonny said, glancing at the hazy sun sparkling on the water. The fog that had been forecast hadn't arrived yet and it was a pleasant morning.

"We could look for them now," said Miriam, who had placed her napkin flat on the table and was loading it with uneaten pastries and cakes from the stand.

Alice nodded. "Yes. Let's go right away."

"What are you doing with those cakes? You can ask for fresh ones whenever you please," said Sonny.

High spots of colour sprang to Miriam's cheeks. "I must look after Mami and Papi in the cabin. I'll take them some cakes for breakfast, then we look for the Frasers."

Chapter 15

THE BAG

The three children began their hunt for the Frasers on Promenade Deck. While still warm, the increasingly hazy sun meant many people were enjoying the shelter of the covered deck. Alice had been concerned that the three of them together would be noticed, as there were not many children their age on board, but she soon realized that they were wearing the greatest disguise of all; one of ordinariness.

They sidled past passengers snoozing in steamer chairs, reading or chatting over morning coffee served by waiters in bow ties as Miriam focused on locating the Frasers.

"I'm off to the barber shop for a shave," a man said to his friend as they walked past. "I'll see you at the tennis nets later on."

"Let's go to the cinema tonight. I hear they are showing the latest Fred Astaire film," replied the friend.

Alice nudged Sonny. "Fred Astaire is on board right now. I saw him doing a tap dance on this deck yesterday – can you imagine!"

Sonny grinned. "That's nothing. Last week Johnny Weissmuller – the actor who plays Tarzan in the films – came to watch our swimming lesson. He's a swimming champ himself and even dived off the top balcony into the pool while we cheered him on."

"I would like to have seen that," said Miriam, grinning too. "Johnny Weissmuller is so brave. Papi said he saved eleven people from drowning after a boat accident in America."

Alice thought with a pang how Gloria would love hearing these stories and made a mental note to jot them down in her adventures scrapbook so they could chat about them at school. She then turned her attention back to Miriam, who had agreed to cough loudly if she saw the Frasers. She remained disappointingly silent, however, as she stared at each passenger in turn.

Continuing on, Alice saw a man with a camera and another with a notepad approach two women who were sitting taking tea. "We're from *The Times* newspaper. Can we interview you about the *Queen Mary's* race for the Blue Riband trophy?" the man with the notepad enquired.

"Oh yes," replied one of the women, leaning forward enthusiastically. "I feel sure the ship will win it."

"Unless this predicted fog slows us down," her friend said a little gloomily.

"Let's hope not. People at home are on the edges of their seats waiting for news," said the journalist as he flipped open his notepad, licked the end of his pencil and began to scribble notes.

Alice felt a pinch of concern at the impending fog and thought of her father and the captain in the wheelhouse. Surely the ship would be forced to slow down if the weather worsened?

"Let's try looking for the Frasers on Sun Deck next," suggested Sonny, after they had completed a full circuit of Promenade Deck.

The breeze whipped Alice's hair around her cheeks as they emerged into the fresh air. She quickly scanned the deck, looking for any sign of her father. Even though he had allowed her to walk around up here, how happy would he be that she had made friends? Maybe he would think them a bad influence, encouraging her to explore areas that were forbidden. Keeping a close eye out for him, Alice followed the others towards the stern, soon arriving at the Verandah Grill restaurant. She gazed longingly at its circular bay windows and varnished wooden door, wishing they could linger and take a look inside. In this restaurant reservations had to be made months in advance; it was a place to see and be seen.

"Quick...look," said Sonny, tugging on Alice's cardigan sleeve.

Alice turned, wondering if he had caught sight of the Frasers, but saw he was pointing out to sea. Her breath hitched in her throat as she spotted a small pod of dolphins grazing the wake, dancing and diving as they followed the ship.

Miriam clutched her arm. "They are wonderful," she whispered.

"They're white-sided dolphins," said Sonny, whose eyes were glued to the spectacle. "You can tell by the stripe on their side. This is the best thing about being out at sea. Spotting birds and sea life."

Alice continued to watch the pod until they disappeared, thinking that Sonny was right. The magnificence of the ocean was far more impressive than seeing inside a fancy restaurant.

Miriam gave a sudden loud cough and nodded upwards.

Above the Grill was another area of deck. Two people lay on steamer chairs, so low their faces were hidden, but the tip of the man's straw Panama hat and the woman's red-and-blue scarf were clearly visible. The Frasers! Alice felt a flutter of anticipation. Was that the man responsible for hurting Joseph? She fingered the tip of the paper with the suspects' names in her dress pocket.

Miriam pointed at the steps. "We must go up there. Then you can listen to them speaking."

"Yes," said Alice determinedly.

"But it would look suspicious if we all go," said Sonny, scrunching his nose.

Alice nodded. "Yes, you're right. How about you see if you can find out anything about the Blakes on A Deck while Miriam and I investigate the Frasers," she suggested.

"You'll have to keep hidden," said Sonny, looking worried. "Mr Fraser might recognize Miriam from when she bumped into him earlier."

"Don't worry. We'll be fine," said Alice, trying to sound confident.

"Yes. We will be fine," echoed Miriam, who was looking up at the Frasers with interest.

Sonny still didn't look too thrilled at the plan but agreed to meet them in an hour at Charlie's lift to exchange information.

Waving goodbye, Alice pushed her shoulders back and set off with Miriam to see what they could find out.

Finding a sheltered spot between two large white air vents to observe the Frasers, the girls settled down to wait in the hazy sun. It was quite warm and peeling off her cardigan, Alice tied it round her shoulders.

They soon realized why so few people had chosen to sit on this part of the deck. The ship's funnels belched out oily smoke, smuts peppering the air and deck like black snow. A large smoke smut landed on Alice's dress. She rubbed at it, and it smudged.

Another floated onto Miriam's arm. She licked a finger and wiped it away.

As they dealt with the smuts, they both quietly watched the Frasers. Mrs Fraser was avidly flicking through the pages of a fashion magazine while Mr Fraser dozed, his head lolling to one side. They would have to wait for him to wake up before they could hear his voice. Every so often Mrs Fraser would sweep the smuts from her magazine and clothes, bristling with irritation, as their large bag rested between them on the deck.

Something occurred to Alice. "Why have they chosen here when they could easily sit ahead of the funnels away from the smoke smuts?" she whispered to Miriam.

Miriam shrugged. "It is strange, yes." She gave Alice a curious glance. "I would like to know more about Sonny's friend and why we watch these people."

Alice pulled her knees to her chest, wrapping her arms round them. Miriam had helped them find the Frasers with intent and gusto. She deserved to know the full truth. Alice quickly recounted the argument she had overheard in the swimming pool; Joseph being pushed down the steps and the hidden package they had found and what was inside it. She finished by pulling the paper from her pocket with the details from the passenger manifest and explaining how the Blakes and the Frasers seemed the most likely culprits. "We must find out who did this to Joseph before the ship gets to New York and they have a chance to escape."

Miriam's expression hardened as she studied Alice's note. "I will help find the person who hurt Joseph. They must be stopped."

"Thank you," said Alice with a grateful smile.

Alice looked again at the Frasers' bag. Mrs Fraser had placed a blanket over it, anchoring the bag under the feet of their chairs. Was this to protect whatever was inside from the sun – or from prying eyes?

Alice shifted position, her legs aching. Mrs Fraser's magazine had fallen to one side, and she was dozing now too. There had been no conversation and the urge to see what was inside the bag was becoming like an itch Alice could not scratch. But there was no way to find out without disturbing them.

Miriam suppressed a yawn and Alice rested her head back against the vent as she wondered what to do next.

"*Ein hund!* A dog!" whispered Miriam in amazement, as the unexpected sound of scampering feet made Alice look down.

She saw, to her huge surprise, a small brown sausage dog an arm's length ahead of them. Animals weren't allowed on the ship apart from in the kennels. Had the dog escaped from there? But she didn't remember seeing this one yesterday when she'd visited the kennels with Sonny.

The dog ambled over and sniffed Miriam's hand. She grinned. "Where is it from?"

It struck Alice then how absurd this was. They weren't in a local park, or a village street.

The dog turned its attention to Alice and gave her hand a tickly lick. She stifled a laugh and watched it scuttle across the deck.

She glanced back at the Frasers and noticed something curious. "Look," she said to Miriam, pointing at the bag. The blanket covering the bag had lifted to reveal a wide opening.

"They keep a dog in their bag?" asked Miriam, her eyes widening.

"Maybe. This is our chance, it gives us an opportunity to start a conversation with them," said Alice, hoping to hear Mr Fraser's voice at last.

Miriam nodded and they crept after the animal, crawling panther-like over the smoke-smutted wood, Alice's bare knees quickly becoming grubby.

Reaching out, Alice gently reached for the dog, while Miriam approached from the other direction in case it ran off. The animal didn't seem at all disturbed to be in Alice's arms and it snuffled her fingers.

"Good dog," said Miriam softly, tickling it behind the ears.

Alice saw Mr Fraser yawning widely and stretching.

He glanced at the empty bag and a look of alarm crossed his face. He shook his wife awake.

"Come on," said Alice, the dog wriggling against her chest as they hurried over to the couple.

"Oh!" exclaimed Mr Fraser, jumping to his feet as Alice and Miriam approached. Spots of colour flushed his cheeks, and he gave his flustered wife an anxious glance.

Mrs Fraser held out her arms. "Pixie. My darling Pixie."

Alice passed Mrs Fraser the dog and watched and waited as the couple settled the animal into the bag and gave it a biscuit to munch on. She stared at Mr Fraser's florid cheeks, wondering if, when he spoke, it would reveal that he was the person who had pushed Joseph. Her heart cantered in her chest, and she stood a little closer to Miriam, glad she was not facing him alone.

"Thank you," said Mr Fraser. "This must seem a little irregular, but we can explain."

Alice felt her heart begin to slow. Mr Fraser had a deep voice and spoke with an American accent. She glanced at Miriam and gave a small shake of her head. This was not the man who had pushed Joseph.

"Hey, I recognize you. You're the girl who bumped into us earlier in the passageway," Mr Fraser said, looking at Miriam.

Miriam stepped backwards; perhaps afraid he would shout again.

"I am sorry I shouted. I felt bad about that afterwards. Pixie was in the bag and I was afraid you'd find out our secret," Mr Fraser said. "I truly am sorry."

A look of relief crossed Miriam's face and she nodded.

"Our beloved Pixie is old and becomes anxious when she's apart from us. She refuses her food if we're not there," explained Mrs Fraser, who was British. Her voice was threaded with worry. "We've been back and forth to Britain these past few months as my father is unwell," she continued. "We couldn't leave Pixie at home in Massachusetts. It just wouldn't have been right. And we couldn't bear to put her in the ship's kennels knowing she would be so unhappy."

"You won't tell anyone, will you? Pixie doesn't bark. She's a good girl," pleaded Mr Fraser.

Alice saw the dog's soft brown velvety nose push out of the bag and she smiled, thinking of Rocket bouncing around in his cage in Sonny's cabin.

"I understand why you must be with your dog. We will keep her a secret," said Miriam firmly and Alice nodded her agreement.

"Thank you. I should have kept a closer eye on her, but

we're just so tired after the arguing last night from the tiresome couple next door," sighed Mrs Fraser, as she fed Pixie another dog biscuit and Mr Fraser folded the blanket.

Alice's fingers tingled. The Blakes' cabin, A98, must be close to the Frasers'. Could it be that the Frasers were talking about them? She racked her brains for how they could find out more. Before Alice had a chance to order her thoughts, Miriam pushed her shoulders back and stepped forward.

"My cabin is on A Deck also. Please…what is the name of these people who disturb you?" asked Miriam boldly, giving Alice a quick glance.

"Mr and Mrs Blake. Have they kept you awake too?" asked Mr Fraser eagerly.

Miriam shook her head, then turned to Alice and raised her eyebrows.

Alice stiffened. It *was* the Blakes the Frasers had overheard arguing!

"My husband had to ask them to keep the noise down last night," Mrs Fraser said in disgust.

"At least Mr Blake apologized," said Mr Fraser. "Although the chap practically slammed the cabin door in my face as his wife was on the telephone by the time I went round."

"Imagine them arguing about diamonds too! Some

people have real problems to worry about. We should report them if we get a repeat of that tonight, or we'll get no sleep on this voyage at all," said Mrs Fraser haughtily.

"It was nice to meet you, but we really should go," said Alice tugging on Miriam's arm. Saying goodbye to the couple, they slipped away down the steps, Alice's head buzzing. "Well done finding that out about the Blakes, Miriam. You're a quick thinker!"

Miriam shrugged quite casually. "I saw the Blakes' cabin number on your note. I also see it must be close to the Frasers' cabin. Papi says it is important to never stop asking questions."

Alice grinned, thinking that was jolly good advice. While they had successfully eliminated the Frasers from their list of suspects, they had uncovered something else interesting instead: the Blakes had been arguing late at night about diamonds. Alice and Miriam needed to meet up with Sonny and Charlie to tell them what they had learned at once.

Chapter 16

INVESTIGATIONS

Charlie grinned at Alice and Sonny as the doors to his lift opened, his eyes widening at Miriam. Swift introductions were made as Charlie ensured they glided up and down in the lift without stopping, giving Alice a chance to explain everything. She told Charlie about Pixie the dog and how her escape had given her a chance to listen to Mr Fraser's voice and discover he was not the person who had pushed Joseph.

Sonny looked shocked. "I'm not the only one with an animal secret then."

Miriam gave him a quizzical look.

"He has a pet mouse on board," whispered Alice.

Miriam shrugged as if this was perfectly acceptable.

"It explains why Mr Fraser was so angry when you bumped into his bag. He was afraid you would discover his secret," said Sonny thoughtfully.

Miriam looked offended. "I can keep secrets."

"I'm sure you can," said Alice with a smile.

"I went to the hospital again this morning. Joseph is no better," said Charlie grimly. "I pressed the nurse for information, and she said...she said the doctor doubts he will wake up at all."

Sonny dipped his head in dismay.

Alice's stomach swooped unpleasantly. "That's dreadful," she said.

"Poor Joseph," Miriam said in a hushed voice.

They stood in silence for a few seconds and a fresh anger at what had happened to Joseph made Alice's jaw clench. "We must do all we can to get justice for him. Miriam and I found out some things that may help with that," she said, explaining how the Frasers had heard the Blakes in the next-door cabin arguing about diamonds.

"Diamonds!" said Sonny excitedly. "Could this be connected to the gold ingot and note hidden under my mattress?"

"Perhaps the Blakes are paying this R to steal jewellery?" suggested Alice.

"But it would have to be many diamonds to make it worth more than the gold ingot. And anything *that* valuable is kept in the ship's safe," said Charlie with a frown.

"They break the safe and steal all of the diamonds?" suggested Miriam.

"Impossible. It would be like trying to get into the palace to visit the king," said Charlie, polishing the lift's brass control panel.

Alice tilted her head to the ceiling and let out a heavy sigh. This conversation was getting them nowhere. "We don't even know if the Blakes are after diamonds yet. I really need to hear Mr Blake's voice. That will at least tell us if he is the person who hurt Joseph."

Sonny wrinkled his nose. "That might be difficult. I spoke with a steward on A Deck. The Blakes stay in their cabin most of the day. He's only seen them come out for dinner."

"But why stay inside when there's so much to enjoy on the ship?" mused Charlie, rubbing at another smudge on the wall.

"They are hiding something," said Miriam firmly.

"We need to think of another way of investigating

Mr Blake then," said Alice, recalling one detail from her conversation with the Frasers that could help. "Mrs Blake was making a phone call when Mr Fraser asked them to keep the noise down last night. He said Mr Blake seemed awfully keen to get rid of him."

"Which makes me think Mr Blake didn't want the call to be overheard," said Sonny, folding his arms.

"Perhaps his wife was speaking with R?" suggested Alice. "How do telephone calls work on the ship? Is there a way of finding out who she was speaking to?"

Charlie looked at Sonny. "What about asking Bernard? He's in our swimming group and works in the telephone operations room. Records are kept of all internal calls, and ship to shore calls must be booked in advance and are taken in the telephone booths on Promenade Deck. He might be able to tell us who the Blakes spoke to."

"At last, a plan," said Miriam with a grin.

Alice felt a glow of satisfaction. It was good to be making progress and working as a team, but she couldn't shake off the image of Joseph lying in a hospital bed with his eyes closed. The urgency with which they needed to solve this was only rising.

"Bernard finishes around three o'clock. I'll get a message to him saying you'd like to meet straight after," said

Charlie, slowly folding his cloth. He looked up. "I have to get back to work. Don't have too much fun investigating without me."

"Don't worry. We're in this together. We'll report back anything we discover," said Alice.

Charlie's cheeks flushed with pleasure and Sonny reached up and tweaked his hat to one side.

Miriam laughed. The sound was high and hopeful, and it made the rest of them laugh too.

Alice's father bolted down his cheese-and-pickle sandwich that lunchtime, chatting about the ongoing race and the captain's reluctance to maintain full speed if the anticipated fog appeared later that afternoon. "This ship is full to the brim with press and photographers. They're sending daily reports to wireless stations across Britain and abroad. We're more than halfway and cannot disappoint the passengers or the people at home waiting for news. Crossing the Atlantic in the fastest time is *all* that matters."

Alice felt he said the last words quite fiercely, as if there was something more on the line for him personally than a job promotion. She remembered what Charlie had said about her father's visits to the ship's hold, and the luggage keys hidden in his desk. Speaking with the Frasers that morning had given her a new confidence and it was time to get answers to some of her questions. Watching her father carefully, she took a small bite of her own sandwich. "It must have been such fun travelling at sea with mother all those years ago."

"Mmm," was her father's response, as he wolfed down the last of his bread and wiped his hands on his napkin.

"I wish there were some of mother's things from that time I could look at. Belongings. Like her clothes perhaps," said Alice, thinking of the silk glove lying in her suitcase and the possibility of her mother's luggage being stored in the ship's hold.

Her father pushed his plate to one side and gave Alice a sorrowful look. "I'm sorry. I...gave your mother's things away after she died. It was a terribly sad time. Maybe that was wrong of me." The worry lines between his eyebrows were deeper than ever.

Alice felt sure he was telling her the truth. But how could that be when the luggage tag in his drawer pointed to the fact her mother's trunks were on board this ship?

"There is enough to keep you entertained on this voyage, isn't there, Alice? Have you enjoyed the library books? I was worried it would be a little dull," her father said, standing up and putting on his jacket.

"Oh, don't worry. I'm not finding it dull at all," said Alice, glad there was at least one thing she could be truthful with him about.

Chapter 17

DIAMOND

Just as her father had predicted, the weather was closing in, and a soup-like mist hung in the air that afternoon, as Alice waited with Miriam and Sonny for Charlie's friend Bernard outside the telephone operations room. The ocean was flat calm though, the only sea spray caused by the ship itself as it steamed onward.

"The ship is going very fast, Papa," said a young boy standing at the railings nearby.

Alice saw the man's face clench. "Yes. We're heading into sea fog too. I hope the captain knows what he's doing."

The young boy turned, concern tightening his own cheeks.

"Don't worry, lad. I'm sure all will be well," said the boy's father, throwing a quick glance at the lifeboats hanging on their cradles.

"Is it safe?" whispered Miriam.

Alice's palms were suddenly clammy at the thought of the potential risk her father and the captain were taking by pushing the ship harder and faster than it had ever gone before. She had to trust they wouldn't risk the passengers' safety. "I'm sure it is," she said, keen to put her friend at ease.

"Hello," said a tall boy stepping out of the operations room.

"Hello, Bernard. Thanks for agreeing to help," said Sonny.

Bernard shifted from foot to foot, a nervous energy radiating from him as he passed Sonny a folded piece of paper. "I'll lose my job if anyone finds out I've given you this information," he whispered, looking around furtively. "I can tell you that the people you enquired about from cabin A96 did make a call and..." His face tightened. "Oh bother... The staff captain is coming this way. He's early. He's come to report to the press back home on the ship's progress."

Alice's heart thumped extra hard and she swivelled to see her father striding along. He frowned as he peered out to sea at the fog. "He mustn't see me here either," she said desperately.

Bernard gave her a quizzical look.

"We'll go to my cabin," said Sonny, ushering Alice and Miriam forward and giving Bernard a nod of thanks.

Alice chanced a quick look back to see her father disappearing into the telephone operations room. He looked preoccupied, his face drawn. Was this because of the fog or something else? She thought again of the keys to her mother's trunks, his mysterious visits to the hold and the detective bureau card. He was keeping secrets and she needed to find a way to uncover them.

Threads of mist pressed against the portholes of Sonny's cabin, as Miriam fussed over Rocket and Alice sat on the bunk. Unfolding Bernard's note, Sonny stood before them and read it out loud.

Last night at 23.15 hours the occupants of cabin A96 telephoned the operations room to book a ship to shore call with the Diamond Shipping Company. This will take place tomorrow, Sunday 26th July, at 0900 hours in telephone booth two on Promenade Deck.

"The Diamond Shipping Company?" said Alice with surprise.

"The Blakes weren't arguing about real diamonds at all," said Sonny.

"What is this Diamond company?" asked Miriam, scrunching her nose.

"It's an American company which has built some jolly fast ships, like the *Sapphire*," said Sonny. "I remember my grandfather telling me about it. He was quite fascinated by shipping. He even had a small yacht of his own, not that I ever got to see it."

Sonny's words brought a memory of something her father had said swimming to the front of Alice's mind: *There are many rivals out there who would dearly love us to lose the race, like the current holder of the trophy, the* Sapphire. *We can't have that, can we?*

She was struck by a terrible thought. "The *Sapphire* is currently the fastest ship on the seas. What if...what if the Blakes are on board to stop her record from being beaten?"

"You mean stop the *Queen Mary* from crossing in a faster time?" asked Sonny, his brow wrinkling as he looked at Bernard's note again.

"Charlie said the winner of the race gets more contracts and passengers. Then there is the prestige. They must all be incentives for Diamond Shipping to want to keep the trophy. If the Blakes have some connection to Diamond, that might give them a reason to try to sabotage the *Queen Mary*'s crossing," said Alice, going on to tell them exactly what her father had said.

Sonny frowned. "Just suppose you are right, how would the Blakes stop this ship from winning the race? And how does that connect to R and the gold ingot?"

"The Blakes have had time to make a plan," said Miriam, as she fed Rocket a sunflower seed. He held it in his paws and nibbled.

"Exactly. They've been on the ship many times and have had time to make contacts, like Joseph. The package of gold he was supposed to give to R must be part of the plan," said Alice.

"They give R gold to stop the ship?" suggested Miriam, looking up.

Sonny puffed out a breath. "Ships can't just be stopped. Someone would need to meddle with the controls to make that happen."

"Maybe that's what R is planning. It's why they needed someone on the crew," insisted Alice. The thought that someone who worked with her father might betray him this way made the back of her neck flash hot.

Miriam frowned as Rocket scampered down her skirt and plopped onto the carpet. She dropped to her knees to follow the mouse on his exploration of the cabin. "We must listen to the Blakes' telephone conversation with Diamond Shipping tomorrow. That will tell us more."

Sonny's eyebrows pulled together. "Good point. It will also mean Alice can hear Mr Blake's voice and hopefully identify him as the man who pushed Joseph."

Alice shivered at the memory of Joseph's sharp intake of breath as he was pushed down the steps. What Sonny was saying made sense, but there was a problem. "What if *Mrs* Blake makes the telephone call? We'll have wasted valuable time waiting to hear his voice when we could have been working on other ways to confirm what he's up to."

"I suppose," said Sonny. "But the Blakes might have already put their plan into action! We could be too late."

"No. My father said the race is going well. He's a bit worried about the fog, but the Blakes can't influence that. Whatever this plan is of theirs, it hasn't got going yet," said Alice.

"We need evidence of the Blakes' plan," said Miriam firmly.

"Miriam is right," Alice said, staring at Sonny's cabin key lying beside Rocket's cage. An idea had struck her.

"We search for evidence in the Blakes' cabin," said Miriam, following Alice's gaze.

"Yes," said Alice, smiling at the way Miriam's thoughts often seemed to mirror her own.

"But...no," said Sonny incredulously, taking Rocket from Miriam and settling him into a nest of shredded newspaper in his cage. "You can't just enter the Blakes' cabin without permission."

"If the Blakes are helping Diamond Shipping sabotage the *Queen Mary*'s race, there must be evidence in their cabin to prove it. Something that could lead us to R and firmly link them to Joseph."

"It's far too risky," said Sonny, shaking his head.

"You worry too much about breaking the rules," said Alice, tilting her own head.

Sonny flushed a deep pink as he shut the cage door. "And you don't worry enough," he muttered.

"When we left Germany, it was a risk," said Miriam softly. "But it was worth it. It is also a risk to prove the Blakes are bad people, but we must take that risk."

"And it's a risk worth taking if it will help Joseph," said Alice firmly, her scalp prickling at Sonny's remark. She did worry – her father's declaration that he wanted "no dramas or distractions" rang hollow in her ears – but they had to get answers to this puzzle, and fast.

Sonny gave a resigned sigh and shook his head. "I can see neither of you will change your minds on this." Miriam and Alice exchanged a conspiratorial grin. "I suppose you have a plan for getting into the Blakes' cabin?" he continued, folding his arms.

"Well we know they go for dinner each night, so their cabin will be unoccupied for at least an hour at around seven o'clock," said Alice.

"We'll need a key," said Miriam decidedly, dangling her own cabin key in the air.

"But you need *the Blakes'* key," said Sonny, who still seemed intent on placing obstacles in their way.

Alice took Miriam's key and lay it in her palm, remembering her visit to the room for officers' stewards with Pearl. "But we don't need the Blakes' key. I know where a master cabin key is kept. I can borrow that."

Sonny groaned. "Alice. That's not borrowing, that's stealing. What if your father found out?"

For some reason Sonny's anxiety only fuelled Alice's enthusiasm for this new plan. "I know where spare stewardess uniforms are kept too. I could disguise myself, creep in while the Blakes are at dinner. No one would ever know."

"We can keep watch outside," said Miriam with a grin.

"Yes! This is the right thing to do, I'm certain of it! We'll do it this evening," said Alice.

There was the sound of a door opening and footsteps in the living area of Sonny's suite.

Alice looked at Sonny and Miriam in alarm.

"It's Dorothy. She's returned early," whispered Sonny, standing up and pushing Bernard's note into his trouser pocket.

Alice stood up too, feeling a rush of uncertainty at meeting Sonny's governess. What if she started asking awkward questions?

Alice and Miriam followed Sonny into the living area to see Dorothy turn on the electric fire, which bathed the room in an orange glow.

Dorothy straightened and turned, smoothing the skirt of her stylish cream dress. Her eyes widened at the sight of them and she placed a hand to her throat. "Sonny?" she said uncertainly.

"I've made some friends. This is Alice and Miriam," said Sonny.

Dorothy's blue-grey eyes settled on Alice. The woman's cheeks were a little sunken, and her hair limp, as if she hadn't ventured outside or eaten a hearty meal in a long time. She was a faded version of the person Alice had seen in the photograph in Sonny's cabin.

Alice squirmed as Dorothy's gaze lingered on her. She noticed the smut stains on her own clothes. Maybe Dorothy thought she wasn't suitable company for Sonny. Most of her father's earnings went on her school fees and the upkeep of Aunt Laura's cottage. At the start of each term Alice's aunt grew a little flustered as she assessed which parts of Alice's school uniform were too small and whether her monthly budget would cover replacements. Sometimes that meant purchasing items second-hand, but Alice didn't mind; she felt confident enough to stand up to any barbed comments from mean-spirited girls about hand-me-downs. But Sonny had a different life entirely, one of privilege and wanting for nothing.

"You're on board with your parents?" Dorothy asked Alice haltingly, fiddling with the cuffs of her cardigan.

Alice glanced at Miriam, wondering why only she had been singled out. "Just my father," she said.

"Her father works on board. He's the..." began Sonny. He paused, a crimson flush bursting onto his cheeks as he realized his error.

Alice groaned internally, hoping Dorothy wouldn't press her on who her father was.

There was a long pause, as Dorothy continued to study Alice. Her face looked quite stricken for some reason and she did up the buttons of her cardigan, her fingers fumbling as if she had lost all feeling in them. She turned to Sonny. "I don't think you should get too attached to anyone on this ship. I've decided we should disembark in New York. I'll go to passenger services and see about planning for our departure. We've been on the *Queen Mary* for long enough."

Sonny's jaw twitched. "But...you haven't mentioned this before."

Dorothy flicked her eyes to Alice, then away again. Her bottom lip was trembling.

The odd silence hanging over the cabin was broken by the regular boom of the ship's foghorn.

Sonny looked at his shoes, clearly embarrassed and a little worried.

Alice and Miriam exchanged an uncertain look. "We should leave," said Alice.

Miriam nodded her agreement. "It was nice to meet you," she said, boldly holding out a hand to Dorothy.

Dorothy took Miriam's hand, and the smile she gave her was warm and quite different to the look Alice had received.

Chapter 18

THE BARONESS

Hurrying back to her cabin, Alice pushed thoughts about Dorothy's behaviour, and the pang she felt at Sonny leaving the ship so soon, to one side, for she had hoped they would both be travelling back and forth over the summer.

She had to retrieve the master key and a clean stewardess uniform so they could search the Blakes' cabin that evening. There was only one first-class dinner sitting, at seven o'clock, as the restaurant could accommodate all eight hundred passengers. That also meant first-class areas of the ship would be quiet and gave them a much better chance of sneaking around unnoticed.

Stepping out onto Promenade Deck, Alice was struck by how dense the cold, swirling fog had become. It was just after four o'clock, yet it seemed darkness was falling already. The area that had previously been so full of life was now eerily quiet, many passengers retreating to warmer parts of the ship. The ship's foghorn continued to blast periodically, echoing off the teak deck and long windows.

A lone woman sat in a steamer chair, a rug pulled over her legs as she read her book. She glanced up as Alice walked by, looking worried. "Weather's taken a turn for the worse. The ship doesn't seem to have slowed down though."

Alice stopped and glanced out of one of the long windows. It was impossible to see anything, but the vibrations and roll of the vessel indicated they were still travelling at speed.

"My husband's quite concerned. He even made me try on my lifebelt earlier," the woman continued, clasping her book to her chest. "Make sure you have your lifebelt close to hand tonight."

Alice gave the woman a wan smile and pressed on, thinking of her father in the wheelhouse and Pearl's safety briefing. She wondered if she would remember how to secure the bulky lifebelt with its complicated ties and find a lifeboat, if it came to that. She suddenly felt a little alone and afraid as she hurried on up the steps to Sun Deck.

The clammy mist grasped unpleasantly at Alice's hair and skin as she emerged into the open air. She could barely see two strides in front of her. Turning towards the ship's prow, she made her way slowly along the deserted deck, her fingertips using the damp railing as a guide.

The ship's foghorn boomed, and Alice paused, her pulse beating in her throat. The sound was a warning to any other ships that could be in their path, and she knew it could be heard ten miles distant. All the same, she wished her father was less busy so his calm confidence could confirm their safety.

All of a sudden, a figure in black emerged from the mist. Alice clenched the wooden rail and came to an abrupt halt. A peculiar sound was coming from the person's feet as they stood there, a twittering and clicking. A brief break in the fog exposed a woman dressed head to toe in black chiffon, with a fine array of red and blue jewels round her neck. The woman peered at Alice. The twittering grew more frantic. "Rose?" she said questioningly.

Alice's heart fluttered at hearing her mother's name. She did not believe in ghosts or spirits but, for a second, she wondered if she was mistaken, and this person was an apparition.

"Oh, do be quiet, Basil," the vision in chiffon muttered then, glancing at her feet, both breaking the moment and grounding Alice in reality.

Alice noticed a domed birdcage by the woman's silver shoes. The dart of yellow inside the cage made Alice remember the birds she had seen loaded onto the ship. She felt her heart steady again. This was no ghost; it had to be the baroness and her canaries.

The baroness turned back to Alice. "Forgive me. Now the fog has cleared a little I can see I was mistaken. You're far too young to be Rose."

The air around Alice felt thick. "My mother's name was Rose," she said hesitantly.

The baroness took a step closer. She frowned, her wrinkles deepening. "Was she a seamstress?"

"Yes," whispered Alice, wiping her damp palms on her dress.

"That explains it. You have very similar features to your mother. She was an exceptional seamstress and mended my beaded gowns perfectly. That is why I remember her so well. I was quite upset after she disappeared," said the baroness, shaking her head.

Alice blinked, feeling a warm glow at knowing that she and her mother were alike. But what did the baroness mean when she said "disappeared"? That was a peculiar way to talk about someone dying.

The baroness turned her attention to the cage again. "Oh, Basil dearest. I thought the sea mist would perk you up. I should ask Crawford to take you inside." Giving an impressive and sharp snap of her fingers, a man in a black suit and white gloves stepped from the shadows as if waiting for this very instruction. He gave Alice a small bow and she recognized him as the butler overseeing the business of getting the canaries on board the ship.

Alice gave him a shaky smile and looked back to the baroness. "When you said my mother 'disappeared', what did you mean exactly?" she asked, feeling timid, but also desperate to learn more.

"Please take Basil indoors," the woman said to Crawford, ignoring Alice's question.

"Of course, baroness. Will there be anything else?" said Crawford with a deferential bob of his head.

"No. Just return immediately to escort me to the Verandah Grill. I must not be late. This early dinner reservation was booked months ago," said the baroness testily.

Everything had taken on a dreamlike quality. The mist,

the baroness and her sparkling jewels, Basil the twittering canary, the butler and talk of dinner reservations. And most of all the mention of her mother. Alice's head swam.

"My dear. You look a little peculiar," said the baroness, peering at Alice so closely that the aroma of the salty mist was replaced with a whiff of her powerful floral scent.

"It's just...you mentioned my mother," said Alice, leaning against the railing. She breathed deeply until her surroundings ceased to spin.

"Yes. She disappeared that day and *you* disappeared with her," said the baroness, her tone a little irritated as if she thought Alice must already know this fact.

Alice's teeth had begun to chatter. She folded her arms around her middle. "What do you mean? When was this?" she asked.

The wrinkles on the baroness's papery skin deepened. "It must have been eleven or twelve years ago. Our ship had arrived in New York. I quite clearly remember seeing your mother being ushered into a motor car. She had a child with her. I didn't know she was married, but then she always struck me as the secretive type. I also remember thinking it was a very grand car for a seamstress to be stepping into." The baroness paused. "I picked up the glove she dropped that day too."

The lump which had sprung to Alice's throat felt the size of a suet pudding. "A glove?" she croaked.

"Yes. Beautiful grey silk with peach roses. I remember it quite clearly. Later that day I handed it to the ship's purser. Now he wasn't one to gossip, and of course neither was I, but he told me your mother would not be returning. Very peculiar business and I was quite cross, as she left one of my gowns unfinished." The baroness glared at Alice then, as if this was her fault and she needed to do something to remedy the situation at once. "And how is your mother? Is she here? On board?"

Alice felt a surge of bewilderment. *She and her mother had left the ship and not returned?* Her father had never mentioned they had spent time apart. What did this mean?

Crawford arrived, and the baroness's face lit up. "Jolly good. Dinner time. I hope lobster bisque is on the menu. A few champagne cocktails will slip down nicely too." She leaned forward until Alice felt the baroness's hot breath on her ear. "I'm spending every penny of my late husband's fortune on travelling the world. The canaries and I are taking a train across America and then it's off to Japan! Do remember me to your mother."

Alice saw Crawford's eyes lift to the sky as if he was

perhaps not looking forward to this journey as much as his employer.

The baroness turned to leave, and Alice wondered what the correct etiquette was for saying goodbye. Should she curtsy perhaps? But she need not have worried for the baroness ignored her completely and shuffled away in a bustle of chiffon, leaving Alice with tumbling thoughts about her past and the image of a dropped grey silk glove on a New York dockside.

Chapter 19

DISGUISE

Making her way along the short passageway to the room for officers' stewards, Alice paused and listened for the squeak of shoes or sound of approaching voices. Aside from the shudder of the ship and the blast of the foghorn, it was quiet. Her head throbbed with the peculiar things she had learned from the baroness. She needed to speak with her father about this – or to try, at least. For now, though, uncovering secrets about her own past would have to wait. It was Saturday evening, and the ship was arriving in New York on Monday. She had to direct her attention towards doing everything they could for Joseph – and proving her theory that the Blakes were planning to sabotage the *Queen Mary's* record-breaking attempt to cross the Atlantic. For that she needed to borrow a uniform and the master key so she could search their cabin.

Satisfied that all was clear, Alice opened the door to the stewards' room and stepped inside. She slipped the brass master cabin key from its hook in the cupboard. She selected a clean stewardess uniform that she judged to be about the right size, and swiftly left. Quietly closing the door behind her and walking briskly back to her cabin, she heard the squeak of approaching footsteps. She paused. How would she explain the uniform she was carrying? She looked for somewhere to hide, but there were no nooks or crannies, only the closed doors of officers' cabins. Seeing no other option, she quickly stuffed the uniform up the back of her cardigan and stood against the varnished wood panelling, just as her father rounded the corner.

"Alice," her father said in surprise.

"Um…hello," she said, her heart racing.

He peered at her. "I came to check on you and found you gone. Is everything all right? You look a little flushed."

"I'm fine. I was just taking a walk…to admire the different types of wood…used on the walls," said Alice, saying the first thing that popped into her head.

"Ah. I see," said her father. His eyes brightened. "The panelling is rather magnificent. Did you know fifty-six different types of wood were used during the ship's construction? I can tell you all about that if you like."

"Um...perhaps later?" said Alice, feeling the uniform slip a little under her cardigan. She squirmed and adjusted her position, hoping it would not fall out altogether onto the floor.

"Oh. Of course," said her father, looking a little crestfallen. He cleared his throat. "I'm afraid I won't be able to dine with you tonight. Visibility is poor and it's all hands on deck, so to speak."

Alice swallowed. "It is safe, isn't it? The ship is still speeding along." The fog had been so thick when she was outside it was as if a net curtain had been hung across the sky.

"Yes, it's quite safe. We have the finest navigational equipment at sea. There is no need to worry," her father replied. He paused and tugged at his shirt collar. "There is something I wanted to ask you. Tomorrow is the final night of the voyage and the Gala Dinner. I must sit at the captain's table – it's most tiresome and I find the food a little rich – but I thought you might like to accompany me? Call it a little thank you for being so good about following my rules." His smile was shy and also hopeful.

Alice had longed for an occasion like this when she'd first come aboard, but it would take up precious time she could use to solve the mystery of what the Blakes were up to. But the thought of spending time with her father in this way was impossible to resist – it might also be an opportunity to tell him about the baroness, and the nagging questions she had about her past. "Yes, that would be very nice," she said, feeling the clothes hidden under her cardigan shift again.

"Good," her father said, a broad smile stretching his cheeks. "Well, I'd better get back. Enjoy looking at the wood, and your reading and embroidery of course, and I'll see you in the morning." He leaned forward and gave her shoulder an affectionate squeeze.

"Thank you. I will," said Alice, feeling the stewardess uniform glide to the floor with a whoosh just as her father rounded a corner and disappeared from sight.

"Let's go over this once more," said Alice, feeling the tip of the master key in her pocket as they stood in Charlie's lift that evening. "Sonny and Miriam will hang around the A Deck passageway just before seven o'clock, to confirm the Blakes leave their cabin for dinner."

"Then, while Alice is searching the cabin for evidence linking Mr Blake to Joseph and a plot to sabotage the race, Miriam and Sonny will keep watch at either end of the passageway," said Charlie. His face fell a little. "I wish I could help too."

"You are helping," said Alice, pulling the pale grey stewardess uniform from the bag she had brought with her. "You've provided us with the perfect meeting place to discuss this mystery and a very important and top-secret changing room service."

Charlie grinned as Alice shrugged the uniform on over her dress.

Miriam quickly helped Alice do up the buttons and fix the starched white hat with hairpins, while Alice adjusted the collar and cuffs.

"Well?" Alice said, doing a twirl.

"It's a little...big," said Sonny.

Alice glanced down and grimaced. He was right. The sleeves were too long, and the skirt almost reached the tops of her sandals. Perhaps it would help to disguise her scuffed shoes, which looked a little out of place.

"It will do," said Miriam, giving Alice a firm smile.

"Here, I'll look after your bag," said Charlie, opening a panel in the lift and stuffing it inside.

"Remember what happened to Joseph – this could be dangerous. If the Blakes do come back, I'll walk past their cabin and say very loudly, 'Terrible weather outside.' That's the signal you must leave straight away," said Sonny, who was looking more anxious by the second.

"Don't worry, Sonny. I know we're breaking lots of rules this evening, but I've a feeling this will all work out just fine," said Alice, trying to quell the churning in her stomach and dearly hoping she was right.

Quickly unlocking the Blakes' cabin door and slipping inside, Alice flicked on the lights and tried to calm her breathing. A boom of the foghorn made her jump and she curled her hands into fists, pushing aside troubling thoughts of hidden ships in the mist and a potential collision at sea.

Stepping fully into the room she saw it was smaller than Sonny's suite, with twin beds, bedside tables, a writing desk and chest of drawers. There was a built-in wardrobe on one wall and a door, which she presumed led to the bathroom. She frowned. The cabin was tidy and bore few signs of occupancy at all.

She headed for the desk to begin her search, seeing only

a box of *Queen Mary* embossed stationery, but they were to be found in every cabin and it was not enough to prove the Blakes had written the note accompanying the gold ingot. Opening the desk drawers, she found them to be empty. Turning her attention to the chest of drawers, she opened each in turn. Empty. Empty. Empty. This was becoming more peculiar by the second.

Alice spun around, thinking of the piles of luggage she had seen lowered into the ship's hold. Most people travelled with multiple suitcases for daywear and evening gowns, toiletries and paperback novels. But there was nothing of that nature to be seen here. It was all unnaturally tidy and neat.

She opened the wardrobe to see one suit jacket swinging in time to the ship's movement and two brown suitcases. Her skin prickled in anticipation as she picked them up. They were heavy. She lifted the catches of the first case. It was locked. She tried the other – also locked. Sighing in frustration she stood up. Everything pointed to the fact the Blakes had something to hide. She had to find a way to see inside their luggage.

Alice hunted for the luggage keys, running her fingers inside every drawer, looking under the bed and even searching the rims of the portholes. The foghorn sounded again, as if a reminder to move on with her search. She checked the small bathroom but there was nothing on display in there either, no perfumes or lipsticks or shampoos or silk robes hanging on the back of the door, only a swimming cap and bathing suit on the edge of the bath and a heap of used towels.

Returning to the bedroom, Alice perched on the edge of the bed feeling glum. The Blakes must have taken the key to the suitcases with them. Her eye caught a glimpse of Mr Blake's jacket swinging gently inside the wardrobe, as if doing a silent and lonely waltz. She stood up. Perhaps Mr Blake wore the jackets on alternate nights to dinner. What if...?

Stepping over to the jacket she felt in its outer pockets. Nothing. She slipped her fingers into the silky lining of the internal pocket and grasped something small and metallic. She pulled out two keys attached to a small ring and felt a surge of triumph. *Not so clever after all, Mr Blake.*

Curling the keys into her palm, she glanced at the cabin door. It was still quiet. Kneeling in front of the wardrobe, she tried the keys in the larger of the two suitcases and found the second one fitted. Inside were a few neatly folded women's blouses and slacks and a toiletry bag. She felt around under the clothes and pulled out a cardboard folder. Now this could be something! Alice sat back on her heels. Her eyes widened as she opened it and read the headline of the newspaper clipping inside.

The Daily Eagle

18th July 1936

BRITISH-MADE SHIP SET TO TAKE THE BLUE RIBAND FROM HER AMERICAN RIVALS!

An unnamed source has said the *Queen Mary* will set a course to cross the Atlantic Ocean in the fastest recorded time and win the Blue Riband race on her next westbound voyage. This will surely upset Diamond Shipping, whose vessel the Sapphire won the trophy earlier in the year and has since seen a huge surge in passenger numbers and profits.

Alice felt victorious as she saw that she had been right, the Blakes did have an interest in the Blue Riband race. Under the clipping she spotted a telegram.

Date: 20th July 1936
To: Mr F. Blake, the Dolphin Hotel, Southampton
From: Mr J. Birtwistle, DSC Ltd, New York

Do whatever necessary if J looks like he'll
expose us.
Speak Sunday 26th about Peggy Thomas.
Make sure R slows her down Sunday night before
handing over second payment.

Alice sucked in a breath at seeing the letters DSC. The
telegram had to be from the Diamond Shipping Company!
The reference to J must also mean Joseph. This telegram
was proof he'd been having doubts about helping the
Blakes and that Mr Blake had thought it necessary to
silence him. Joseph's fall had not been an accident and he
had been lucky to survive. She interpreted the words "*slows
her down*" to mean R did have instructions to sabotage the
Queen Mary on Sunday – tomorrow night! Alice felt a hot
burst of indignation as she thought of her father and his
determination to win the race and create a better future
for them both. He would be devastated to learn of this plot.

She read the telegram twice more and committed the
contents to memory, frowning at the mention of Peggy
Thomas. Who was she and what was her involvement in
all this?

Putting the telegram to one side, Alice looked at the
smaller, unopened suitcase. Her search was taking longer

than expected but she needed to be thorough. Unlocking it and lifting the lid she saw two black, rubbery diving suits. She frowned, wondering what the Blakes would want with those. On top of them lay a small green leather case. It was weighty. Perhaps it contained another gold ingot – the final payment for R?

Flipping open the case's metal catches, Alice drew in a sharp breath. This was no gold ingot. It was a small revolver, with a black handle and shiny silver barrel. Terrified of touching it, she quickly placed it down, the hairs lifting on the nape of her neck. Things had taken a dark and dangerous turn.

"Terrible weather outside," came Sonny's loud voice from the passageway. The signal! *The Blakes had returned.*

Alice looked at the telegram and clipping on the floor beside her. To take them would be dangerous – they might notice them missing. Quickly packing everything away and closing and locking both suitcases, she slipped the keys back into Mr Blake's jacket pocket. Before she could make her exit, the cabin door began to open. Alice froze. She was in a tight spot and could see no way out.

Chapter 20

THE BLAKES

The Blakes' cabin door opened at the same moment Alice had a burst of inspiration. Dashing to the bathroom, she snatched two fresh towels from the rail and held them to her chest, her fingers trembling as she thought of the gun in the locked suitcase.

"I didn't think much of the salmon," said a woman's voice. "The service and food are so much better on the *Sapphire*."

"Yes. The wine was warm tonight too," replied a man in a clipped voice.

Alice's stomach dropped. That was the voice of the man

who had pushed Joseph, she was sure of it. She needed to get out of this cabin at once. Pulling in a deep breath and still clutching the towels, she walked quickly into the bedroom. "Very sorry to disturb you, sir, madam. I've brought in fresh towels," she said, bobbing her head.

Sneaking a quick look at the couple, Alice remembered the swimming cap and bathing suit she had noticed on the side of the bath. She realized with deep unease she had seen Mrs Blake before. This was the woman who had been in the pool when they had looked for the package. The one who had seemed to stare right at her. Mrs Blake's hair was pulled back now, stretching her cheeks unnaturally tight as she fiddled with a single strand of oil-black pearls round her neck. If she recognized Alice, she did not show it, but she looked annoyed as Mr Blake assessed Alice coolly.

"We requested not to be disturbed after dinner," he said, his voice lowering an octave or two.

Alice's cheeks felt warm. "Um. My apologies. I'm new," she murmured, trying to quell the fear in her voice. Dipping her head, she set off for the door, not knowing if it was the movement of the ship causing her legs to shake, or her terror. Hearing Mr Blake's voice had reminded her of how dangerous he was.

"Wait." The instruction from Mrs Blake was forceful and commanding.

Alice felt nausea rise in her throat. She turned slowly.

"Aren't you forgetting something?" Mrs Blake asked, still fiddling with her pearls as she peered at Alice.

Alice blinked. "Um..."

"The towels," barked Mrs Blake in irritation. "You can leave them in the bathroom."

"Oh. Yes," said Alice, quickly returning them to the rail.

The Blakes watched Alice silently as she left. Clicking the cabin door closed with relief, Alice saw Sonny and Miriam standing a little way along the passageway to the right. Their anxious expressions brightened as they saw her.

Alice placed a finger to her lips, and she hurried towards them, keen to put as much distance between herself and the occupants of Cabin A96 as she possibly could.

Charlie was busy delivering passengers to the lounges and bars in his lift after dinner, so Alice, Sonny and Miriam made their way to Sun Deck to find somewhere to talk, Alice removing her uniform disguise in one of the ladies' bathrooms and stuffing it in the dirty linen bin under some used towels on the way.

The ship rose and fell like a person breathing as they walked, and the fog coated everything in a peculiar and salty dampness. Few passengers had ventured out for post-dinner walks in the unfavourable conditions and they found themselves alone.

Ducking between two air vents, Sonny dried a wet bench with his handkerchief, and Alice settled between her two friends to update them on the troubling things she had discovered; that after hearing Mr Blake's voice she was certain he'd pushed Joseph, and that Mrs Blake had been the woman swimming when they'd searched for the package. She told them about the newspaper clipping telling of the rivalry between the *Sapphire* and the *Queen Mary* and the telegram from the Diamond Shipping Company saying R would slow the ship on Sunday evening. It also seemed that the Blakes' telephone call to Diamond Shipping tomorrow would be to discuss someone called Peggy Thomas, who was involved in this too. Lastly, Alice mentioned the revolver.

"A gun," whispered Miriam, alarm tightening her cheeks.

Sonny's face looked chalk-white in the dark. "This is very worrying."

Alice shivered in the cold and tugged down the sleeves of her dress. "Mrs Blake didn't seem to recognize me, but they both saw my face today." The bravery she had felt while searching the cabin had disappeared, leaving a sick feeling in the pit of her stomach.

"You are safe with us," said Miriam firmly, taking one of Alice's hands and giving it a firm squeeze. Alice squeezed back, thankful for the warmth.

"We must tell someone about the gun, Alice," said Sonny, his eyes owl-like.

Alice shook her head. "How can we? The gun on its own won't prove anything and Mr Blake may get into trouble, but it won't stop the plot or help Joseph."

"It would also make Mr Blake angry. He may come after us," said Miriam darkly.

"Miriam's right. Telling someone about this will put us at greater risk," said Alice.

"What a mess," said Sonny glumly. "Your thoughts were right. The Blakes must work for Diamond Shipping. They want to stop the *Queen Mary* from stealing the Blue Riband trophy from their ship the *Sapphire*."

"It's dastardly all right," said Alice. "Joseph must have figured out what they were up to. When he threatened to speak up, Mr Blake did his best to silence him."

Sonny frowned. "But we still don't know how this R plans to tamper with the ship to slow it down."

"There is only one place. The engine room," said Miriam decisively.

"Yes! It's more likely to happen down there than in the wheelhouse. My father and the captain will be watching that place like hawks," said Alice. "That means R could be an engineer. If we find out who he is, maybe we can persuade him not to go along with the Blakes' plan."

"But R could be dangerous too. Why would he switch to our side?" said Miriam.

"He must be annoyed that the Blakes haven't paid him the first instalment of gold as promised," said Alice.

Sonny frowned, thinking hard. "I can't believe I'm suggesting this, but we could use the gold hidden under my bunk to bargain with him? If R wants the gold badly enough, he may decide to help us."

There was a noise to their left, like the slip of feet on damp wood.

Alice stared silently into the dark, her heart skipping. She could see nothing through the shrouds of mist.

"What was that?" whispered Miriam nervously.

"I don't know, but we should go," said Sonny in a low voice. "We'll walk you back to your cabin, Alice."

Alice gave a quick nod. "I'll see if I can locate an R working in the engine rooms on my father's crew list. I'll look for

Peggy Thomas too," she said as they set off.

"Remember Bernard's note," said Miriam. "The Blakes will telephone Diamond Shipping at nine o'clock tomorrow morning from telephone booth two on Promenade Deck. We must listen to that call."

Alice grimaced. "Good idea. That should tell us something about Peggy Thomas. I should probably stay away though in case they recognize me, now they know what I look like." Making a quick plan to meet up with Sonny and Miriam after they had attempted to listen in on the Blakes' telephone call the next day, Alice said goodbye to her friends. They had less than twenty-four hours to bring a halt to the Blakes' ghastly plan and bring justice for Joseph. Time really was running out for them all.

Chapter 21

GONE

Alice slept fitfully, her dreams filled with locked suitcases loaded with small revolvers, shiny gold ingots and cryptic telegrams. She yawned as she pulled back the curtain the next morning, to reveal white puffy clouds, sunshine and a sparkling sea. The ship had successfully steamed through the fog and was on its final run to New York. A record-breaking crossing and the race trophy had to be within the ship's grasp...unless the Blakes had their way.

Kneeling by her bunk and opening her suitcase, Alice took out her adventures scrapbook and read the notes she had made after re-examining both the crew and passenger lists on her father's desk. Frustratingly there was no Peggy Thomas on either list, but she had jotted down the names of the ship's engineers they could investigate further in the hope of finding R and persuading him not to go along with the Blakes' plan.

Cuthbert _Rawlings_ – Boiler Engineer
Andrew _Richardson_ – Junior Engineer
Robert Bell – Second Engineer

She took out her mother's silk glove and held it to her cheek, thinking about the mysteries of her own past that needed solving too and wondered if she would glean any information from her father at the Gala Dinner that evening. But there was no time to be distracted by that now. Putting the glove away, Alice noticed then that an envelope had been slipped under her door. She picked it up and opened it.

Urgent. Come to my cabin at seven-thirty.
I've found out something that will help us.
S.

If her father was surprised to see Alice glance repeatedly

at her watch and wolf down her poached eggs as they ate breakfast in his cabin, he did not show it. Perhaps this was because he was also in a great hurry himself.

"It's the final full day of the voyage, Alice. The worst of the weather is behind us and today we make our final push for the trophy. Just over six hundred nautical miles and twenty hours to go, if we can maintain a speed of thirty knots," he said in delight as he munched on his kippers and toast. "I won't see you at lunch but be ready to leave for the Gala Dinner just before seven o'clock," he continued. "Actually, before I go, I have a small gift for you." He gestured at a W.H. Smith gift bag resting on his bunk.

Alice stepped over to it and looked inside. Pulling out an oblong box she opened it to find a silver pen resting on a maroon velvet cushion. It was slim and cool and fitted the curves of her hand perfectly.

Her father looked uncertain. "Did I choose the right thing? I had wondered about a new scarf, or perfume, but after hearing how you intended to write about our travels, I thought you might enjoy this more."

"It's perfect. Thank you, Father," said Alice, rushing over and throwing her arms round his neck, breathing in the smell of the sea, his aftershave, and a faint whiff of kippers. She swallowed back a surge of guilt at the secrets she was keeping and hoped they would be resolved before he ever found out.

Alice kept her head down as she hurried to Main Deck; she had no desire to come face to face with the Blakes again today. Arriving at Sonny's cabin just after seven-thirty, she was surprised to see the door slightly ajar. She rapped on it, feeling a little nervous about seeing Dorothy again after their strange interaction the previous day, but no one came.

Knocking once more, she tentatively pushed the door open. "Sonny? I came as soon as I..." she began, but the rest of her words she swallowed with a gasp. The cabin was a mess. Chairs had been overturned, desk drawers hung open, books and magazines were strewn across the carpet. There had been a break-in. She threw a desperate look up and down the passageway, but it was early and still quiet.

Alice's pulse thundered in her ears as she thought of two important things – Rocket and the gold ingot hidden under Sonny's bunk. "Hello...is anyone there?" she said tentatively, stepping inside. The cabin seemed to be empty and she crept around the mess to Sonny's bedroom, seeing immediately that Rocket's cage door was open and, more troubling than that, it was empty too.

Dropping to her knees, Alice called out to the tiny mouse. She thought she heard a faint squeak and a rustle under the bed but try as she might she could not catch a glimpse of him or persuade him to come out.

She sat back on her heels feeling desperate. Who would have done this? And where were Sonny and Dorothy? Lifting the mattress, she saw that the package containing the gold ingot and the note Sonny had hidden were gone. Realizing there was nothing she could do to retrieve Rocket, she closed Sonny's door to stop him from escaping and looked again at the suite's dishevelled living area.

Thoughts began to gather like storm clouds in her head as something caught her eye on the low table near the sofa. Spilling from the open lid of the wooden keepsake box was something silky and oddly familiar. She blinked, the item was drawing her forward as if she were being wound in on one of the ship's winches.

Dropping to her knees, she gingerly picked the item up. *A silk glove.* She gently touched the embroidered peach roses with the pad of a thumb and felt a wave of dizziness. It was the twin to the one she had in her suitcase. Looking inside, she saw the familiar embroidered initials: *R.T.* – *Rose Townsend.* She slipped the glove on to her hand. It fitted perfectly. Alice pulled in a deep breath, then another, then another. The thoughts buzzing in her head were like a bee swarm and she closed her eyes.

"Right, you. Stop what you're doing and stand up."

Alice flicked her eyes open to see a steward standing in the doorway, his hands on his broad hips. "I was informed there was a break-in while the passengers of this cabin were at breakfast. We don't tolerate thieving on this ship," he said crossly.

"No. You've got this wrong," croaked Alice, quickly slipping the silk glove up the arm of her cardigan sleeve as the steward gaped at the mess.

He turned back to Alice and looked her up and down. "I know your type. Sneaking up from third class and thieving. You are coming with me," he said officiously. Marching over, he steered Alice out of the cabin.

"But...it wasn't me," she said desperately, her head spinning.

"That's what they all say," the steward replied with a sigh. "Turn out your pockets," he commanded.

Alice did as he asked, keeping her arms close to her body, and hoping the glove would not slip down her sleeve and reveal itself.

The steward gave a dissatisfied grunt to find her pockets empty, as if he'd been hoping to find them stuffed with rubies. "What's your name and cabin number?" he asked.

Alice pressed her lips together, thankful that in her rush to meet Sonny she'd forgotten her cabin key, for it would have revealed who she was.

"There you are, sir, thank you for reporting the crime. We've got the culprit," said the steward.

Alice looked up to see who the steward was talking to and her knees buckled. *The Blakes.* Their faces were as cold as marble as they stared at her. She was hit with a burst of realization as her thoughts settled into place. The note pushed under her cabin door from Sonny... The break-in... The Blakes had set her up. She groaned inwardly as she thought back to the noise she had heard the previous evening while quietly talking to Sonny and Miriam in the mist. The Blakes hadn't been fooled at all by her stewardess disguise and had followed her.

With rising horror, she remembered Sonny speaking of the gold ingot being hidden under his bunk. They had unwittingly led the Blakes straight to the gold. An image of the gun hidden in the Blakes' suitcase sprang into her head and she clenched her teeth to stop them chattering. The fact that they had delivered a note to her cabin must mean that the Blakes had found out who her father was too.

This was a stark and severe warning not to meddle.

"I'm glad we could be of assistance," Mrs Blake said to the steward in a slinky voice that made Alice's skin feel like it was crawling with ants.

"What happens to thieves caught on this ship?" asked Mr Blake mildly.

The steward's jaw tightened. "They are locked in the isolation ward usually reserved for stowaways, or passengers who are found to have an infectious disease. Don't worry. The chief petty officer oversees discipline, and I'll make sure this girl is questioned. Her parents will be told and action will be taken."

"I didn't do it. It wasn't me," Alice said, glaring at the Blakes.

Mr Blake raised an eyebrow. "Can't have criminals *and* liars wandering the ship."

Mrs Blake's lips curled into a whisper of a smile.

As the steward marched Alice along the passageway, anger curdled in the pit of her stomach. It was only eight o'clock in the morning, yet the day had already taken a disastrous turn.

Chapter 22

ISOLATION WARD

Alice lowered her head as the steward marched her down the stairs towards the B Deck isolation ward. She opened her mouth several times to tell him her father was the staff captain and of course she wasn't a thief. But then she thought about what this would mean. Even if her father believed she hadn't broken into Sonny's cabin, he would be cross and highly embarrassed by her behaviour.

The steward unlocked a door marked *Crew only* and gestured for Alice to walk ahead. The passageway was short, curved and narrowed. White metal pipes snaked across the ceiling and vibrations from the ship's powerful propellors thrummed through the walls and floor; they were approaching the very back of the ship.

"Here we are," said the steward, looking at a white door with a round window marked *Women's Isolation Ward*. "Phyllis? I've a thief here for locking up," he called gruffly.

A young woman dressed in a white uniform stepped out of the nurses' station next door. "Oh dear," she said, with a gentle sigh. "How old are you?"

"Twelve," mumbled Alice.

"What cabin are you in? Are you travelling with your parents?" she asked with a kind smile.

Alice looked at the floor, still reluctant to draw her father into this mess.

"Caught her red-handed thieving in a suite on Main Deck," said the steward, rolling his eyes. "There were witnesses too. I didn't find anything on her, but I'm sure I would have done if I'd come along a few minutes later."

Alice glanced up. "I didn't do it," she said fiercely.

The steward gave the nurse a knowing look, clearly not believing her.

The nurse's gaze was gentle. "Tell me who you're travelling with, I'm sure we can sort this out."

Alice clamped her lips shut.

"She's troublesome all right," said the steward, shaking his head.

"I can take it from here," said the nurse to the steward, and Alice sensed a slight frostiness to her tone.

"Be sure to call the chief petty officer and have him question her," the steward said, looking a little aggrieved.

"Of course," said the nurse with a nod.

The steward retreated along the passageway, the crew door clanging shut behind him.

"I really didn't do it," said Alice vehemently. "I'd never steal from anyone. It was my friend's cabin which was broken into. It had already happened when I arrived."

"Which cabin was this? Can you tell me exactly what happened from the beginning?" asked the nurse gently, pulling a pad and pencil from her apron pocket.

"Cabin M73 on Main Deck," said Alice quietly. She chewed on her lower lip, reluctant to tell the nurse about the Blakes and how she was certain they were responsible for the break-in. She didn't want to put herself or anyone else at risk of their anger. They would stop at nothing to get what they wanted; Joseph was evidence of that.

The nurse sighed. "Look. Sit in here and I'll make some enquiries."

Unlocking the door of the isolation ward, the nurse

gestured for Alice to step inside. It was a small and narrow space with four bunks along one wall, two sinks and a porthole. "I'll be back in a short while." Giving Alice another kind look, she closed the door and locked it behind her.

Alice walked over to a bunk and sank onto it with a whump. The sheets were smooth and crisp, and she had a sudden urge to lie down. She felt for the glove up her cardigan sleeve, her eyes prickly with tears. Laying it on the bunk, she ran a thumb over the embroidered roses. All the things she had discovered about her mother and father bubbled up inside, her father's mysterious visits to the ship's hold, her mother's luggage being on board and the detective bureau card she had found. Her mother's gloves. Why would the matching glove to the one in her suitcase be in Sonny's cabin? Racking her brains, she could not think of any explanation for Dorothy or Sonny having it. Could the Blakes have planted it for her to find? But where would they have got it from? Lying on the bunk she closed her eyes, took some deep breaths, and tried to still her frazzled thoughts.

A while later, Alice flicked her eyes open and glanced at the circular window in the isolation room door. The nurse was outside talking to someone, and it sounded like Dorothy. Leaping off the bunk, she strode to the door and listened.

"Thank you for calling me. I'm certain this girl would

not have broken into our cabin. She is a...friend of the child I care for," Alice heard Dorothy say.

"She won't tell me her name," said the nurse. "Which cabin is she travelling in?"

There was a short silence. "Can we please keep this between us? I have a feeling her family would be very disappointed, and I don't want her to get into trouble," Dorothy said with a slight tremor in her voice.

Alice pressed a hand on the door. *Dorothy was trying to get her out.* That was surprising given her lack of warmth when they'd first met.

"Well, I suppose no harm has been done. If you're sure this is just a misunderstanding?" said the nurse.

"Quite sure," said Dorothy firmly. "The purser will investigate the break-in and try and find the real culprit, although from a quick look I can't see anything of value is missing. It is alarming to find out this kind of thing can happen at sea."

Alice strode to the bunk, quickly folded the glove, and pushed it deep into her dress pocket as the isolation ward was unlocked. She turned back to see Dorothy waiting by the door. Her cheeks were creased with weariness.

"Come along," she said gently, ushering Alice from the room.

"Well, goodbye then," said the nurse, escorting them to a door and steps leading to the outside.

Sonny was waiting at the top of the steps, the wind blowing his hair around his strained cheeks. "Are you all right?" he asked Alice, his hand straying to his jacket pocket. She saw a tiny nose sniff the air and retreat.

She nodded. "You found Rocket," she said with relief.

"He's fine, quite upset to be recaptured in fact. The cage door is broken though," said Sonny.

Alice glanced at Dorothy. "Thank you for helping me," she said shyly. "I really did have nothing to do with the break-in."

Dorothy pressed her lips together. "We returned to the cabin after breakfast to find a very officious cabin steward waiting to tell us what had happened. From the description he gave us, Sonny knew he was talking about you. We both knew you would have had no part in the break-in." She glanced at Sonny and swallowed. "Sonny told me who your father is. He said you would get into terrible trouble if he discovered you had been involved somehow." She paused again and rubbed at her neck which was a little blotchy.

"Yes, he would be cross," admitted Alice, making a face.

Dorothy shook her head and looked out at the wake's milky foam as the ship steamed onwards.

"I'll walk Alice back to her cabin," said Sonny.

Dorothy flicked her gaze to Sonny; her cheeks strained with worry. "I've been to passenger services and arranged for us to disembark from the ship when it arrives in New York tomorrow. I'll need help packing later this afternoon."

Alice looked at Dorothy in surprise.

"We're really leaving the *Queen Mary* tomorrow?" asked Sonny his eyes widening. "But where will we go?"

Dorothy threw a furtive glance at Alice that seemed loaded with something unsaid.

Alice sensed Sonny wanted to say more but he stayed silent. She felt the tip of the glove she had found in Dorothy and Sonny's cabin and thought again of the secrets she felt her father was keeping. Then there was Dorothy's odd behaviour around her; spiky one moment then helping to extract her from a difficult situation the next. A peculiar and unsettling feeling sat low in Alice's stomach as it occurred to her that her mother's silk gloves connected them in some way, and she had no idea how.

Chapter 23

MATCHING PAIR

Walking from the isolation ward back to the officers' quarters, Alice filled Sonny in on everything she'd discovered that morning: the message she had supposedly received from him, his cabin being broken into when she arrived, Rocket missing from his cage and the gold ingot and note gone. She told him finally of the Blakes' triumphant faces as she'd been whisked off to the isolation ward by the steward. While bursting to talk to him about the glove too, she decided a quieter moment was needed for that discussion.

"I thought the Blakes must be responsible. I reckon they

overheard us talking on the deck last night, it's the only explanation for them setting you up and slipping that note under your door," whispered Sonny angrily as Rocket sniffed over the top of his pocket. A small girl walking past with her parents saw the mouse and her eyes widened. Sonny paused and fed Rocket a sunflower seed. "The Blakes know who we both are now. They broke into my cabin and tried to have you arrested – and they know we took their gold ingot. We need to stop investigating, it's too dangerous."

"There's still a way we can stop the Blakes. I'm *sure* of it. What about identifying R and trying to persuade him to not go ahead with the plan to sabotage the ship tonight?" said Alice, telling him about the three engineers she had found on the crew list. "Surely it can't hurt to investigate them?"

"But the gold has gone so we've nothing to bargain with," said Sonny. "R is also likely to be as dangerous as the people he is working for. The Blakes have given us a warning not to meddle. They don't worry who they hurt – just look at poor Joseph. Goodness knows what they would do if we continued to look into their activities." He threw a protective glance at Rocket, whose nose and whiskers peeped out of his pocket again.

The sun might have been gleaming on the white-capped waves, but Alice felt a deep and dark glumness at Sonny's attitude. "We can't give up. Let's see what Charlie and Miriam have to say."

"Gosh...Miriam!" said Charlie, checking his watch. "I was supposed to meet her at the telephone booth at nine o'clock to try and listen in on the Blakes' conversation with the Diamond Shipping Company."

"We mentioned the telephone call when we were talking last night. I expect the Blakes overheard us and changed the time," said Alice despondently.

"Perhaps. I completely forgot about it with all the fuss about the break-in – and rescuing you from the isolation ward. I must find Miriam and apologize," Sonny said.

"I wouldn't call it rescuing exactly," mumbled Alice.

Sonny touched her arm and they paused by the railing.

The sun was glaring, and Alice raised a hand to shield her eyes.

"Sometimes things don't work out. You shouldn't feel bad about that," Sonny said, not unkindly.

"But what about getting justice for Joseph and the Blakes' plan to sabotage the ship?" asked Alice. She imagined Mr Blake striding down the gangway the very next day, a smirk on his face, the suitcase containing the gun in his hand. He had to be stopped.

Sonny shook his head. "We can't do anything but hope Joseph wakes up and reports what happened. As for the plan to stop the *Queen Mary* from winning the race, I can't see there is anything to be done."

In the short time Alice had known Sonny, she'd come to see that while he had a cautious nature, he only wanted the best for them all and to keep them safe, whereas her desire for justice was stronger than ever before. She balled her hands into fists, hoping Charlie and Miriam would feel the same.

"I'd better find Miriam and then help Dorothy pack. I wish I knew why we were disembarking tomorrow. Perhaps she's planning on disappearing and leaving me at the dockside," said Sonny, giving Alice a weak smile.

Alice could tell he was secretly very bothered by the situation and wished she could offer words of comfort, but there was something else she needed to speak with him about. "Will you come up to my cabin for a moment? There's something I need to show you."

Sonny frowned. "I let Miriam down. I really should go and find her."

"I'll come with you to look for her. But please do this first. It's very important," said Alice.

"All right then. Just for a few minutes," Sonny replied, throwing Alice a curious look.

Inside her cabin, Alice carefully took the silk glove from her suitcase and placed it on her pillow, all the while watching Sonny for his reaction.

Sonny looked puzzled as he stepped over to the bed. He took Rocket from his jacket pocket and let him scamper up his arm.

Alice then pulled the glove she had found in Sonny's cabin from her dress pocket and placed it by the first. *A matching pair.* It made her feel hot and dizzy to see them reunited.

"I...I don't understand," said Sonny, looking from one glove to the other.

"I found this glove in your cabin this morning. This other one belonged to my mother," said Alice.

Sonny sat heavily on Alice's bunk, the springs creaking in protest. He gawped, his mouth opening and closing, high spots of colour staining his cheeks. "But that's impossible. This glove you've found belongs to Dorothy."

"Dorothy?" asked Alice in surprise.

"Yes. I don't think she's had it long, but I've seen it in her keepsake box," said Sonny.

Rocket ran down Sonny's arm and onto the bed where he sniffed at the gloves, as if curious about them too.

Sonny rubbed his pink cheeks. "What does this mean?"

Alice swallowed, feeling a sudden chill. "You're sure you don't know anything else about the gloves?"

"No. Nothing," said Sonny.

"Maybe...maybe my mother knew Dorothy?" suggested Alice.

"What was your mother's name?" asked Sonny, gently pulling Rocket from the opening to one of the gloves as he attempted to explore inside.

"Rose Townsend," said Alice, pointing out the embroidered initials inside each glove.

Sonny frowned. "I've never heard Dorothy mention that name."

"There's something else that's peculiar," Alice said, going on to tell Sonny about her encounter with the baroness and how the woman had told her that she'd seen Alice's mother drop a glove on the dockside in New York as she was leaving with Alice in a motor car. She also told him about the luggage keys, the *Hope & Son's National Detective Bureau* card she had found and reminded him of what Charlie had said about her father visiting the hold.

"Very peculiar," said Sonny, who seemed to be thinking

hard as he cupped Rocket in his palms. "But I still can't see how Dorothy could be connected to your family. Maybe your mother's luggage contains some answers to this?"

"That's exactly what I wondered too," said Alice. She was surprised to see a small flame building behind Sonny's eyes.

"Perhaps I can help you solve this mystery before I leave tomorrow, especially as Dorothy is involved," Sonny said.

Alice smiled. "You need to know I'm not giving up on the Blakes. I will find a way to stop them. But for now, let's go and find Miriam and then speak with Charlie. I think we need his help getting into the ship's hold."

Chapter 24

LUGGAGE HOLD

A lice and Sonny arrived at Miriam's cabin to find it being cleaned by a cabin steward. "The family have gone to speak with someone about their immigration papers. Mr Brunn expected it to take a couple of hours," he told them.

Seeing they would have talk to Miriam later, the two children thanked the steward and hurried on to the lifts to find Charlie. He whistled through his teeth as Alice updated him on the latest events. "Found a gun, accused of breaking and entering and locked up in the isolation ward. You have been busy."

"I think our investigation into the Blakes must end,

Charlie. It's too dangerous," said Sonny, as the lift they were in glided down.

Alice's fingertips trembled. Recounting everything brought back a sharp memory of the Blakes' leering faces as she was marched off to the isolation ward. They were dangerous, but she had to rise above her own fear. "If we do nothing, the Blakes will get away with what they did to Joseph and ruin the race," she said.

Charlie grimaced. "I agree with Alice. Things have taken a frightening turn, Sonny, but we can't let the Blakes defeat us."

Rocket stuck his tiny nose out of Sonny's pocket, his whiskers twitching as if in agreement.

"I've identified three possible suspects in the engine room who might be R," said Alice, going on to tell Charlie about the information she had gleaned from the crew list.

"Good work, Alice," said Charlie. He paused and turned to Sonny. "Joseph still hasn't woken up. I asked to see him, but the nurse said he's too poorly for visitors," he continued, his eyes watery. "We must act on his behalf; be his voice while he doesn't have one."

"I...just don't know, Charlie," said Sonny, feeding a corn kernel to the mouse.

"Miriam was here earlier," said Charlie suddenly, pulling

out a handkerchief and blowing his nose. "She's got something to tell us about the Blakes but wanted to do it when we were together. Maybe it's something that will help us."

Sonny sighed. "We'll see what she has to say, but I don't reckon I'll be changing my mind on this."

Alice and Charlie exchanged unhappy looks as the lift's mechanism whirred and groaned. Sonny would not change his mind about the Blakes, but he had at least agreed to help solve Alice's own family mystery.

"There's something else you might be able to help us with, Charlie," said Alice, going on to explain about their plan to get into the ship's hold.

Charlie frowned. "Has this got something to do with your father visiting the hold when the ship's in New York?"

"Perhaps," said Alice, quickly telling him about her mother's luggage possibly being stored in there, the detective card she had found, and the story behind the two silk gloves. Any hesitancy she might have felt about sharing this information with him was gone. The only way these secrets would be uncovered was by sharing them.

"That is mysterious. I'm starting to wonder if there's anyone on board this ship who doesn't have a secret," said Charlie, arching an eyebrow. He looked at his watch.

"There might be a way you can get in there, but it will depend on whether the ratcatcher is up to his usual tricks."

"What tricks?" asked Sonny.

"The ratcatcher lets Tiggles, that's the ship's cat, through a hold door on F Deck each day at noon. The cat hunts for vermin and is collected an hour later. That door shouldn't be propped open, but Tiggles yowls if he's shut in," said Charlie.

"Gosh," said Alice, thinking that her father would probably be very unhappy to know a hold door was being propped open. "How has my father not heard about this? And don't the rats escape if the door's left open?"

Charlie shrugged. "This is the *Queen Mary*; there are no rats, but it pays to be sure. Tiggles is well liked by the crew, and his claustrophobia is something the crew are happy to hide."

Alice gave Charlie a wry smile, thinking this was another secret to add to the pile they were already keeping.

"I can get you through the crew door and point you in the direction of the hold. You'll need to duck into one of the storage rooms if you hear anyone coming," continued Charlie. He tilted his head. "Do you think you can do that?"

"We'll give it our best try," said Alice.

"But what if we get caught?" asked Sonny.

"It's a chance we'll have to take," said Alice firmly.

Alice's stomach twisted into an ever-tighter knot as she and Sonny hurried along the F Deck passageway towards the hold. Judders from the engines thrummed through the linoleum floor as they cautiously turned a corner and saw the door directly ahead.

"Alice...I think I've been a little foolish," said Sonny, suddenly looking down.

"Why?" she asked. But as the words left her mouth her question was answered. Rocket had nipped out of Sonny's pocket and was climbing his shirt.

"Goodness, I forgot all about him. And there's going to be a cat in the hold!" whispered Alice.

Sonny gave a meek shrug. "He must have fallen asleep."

Alice felt a rush of worry for the mouse, who she found she was becoming quite fond of. "You'll just have to keep a jolly close eye on him."

As Sonny tried to coax Rocket back into his pocket, Alice saw that something wasn't quite right about the hold door. "It's closed," she said with dismay.

Sonny glanced at his watch as Rocket darted under a

jacket cuff. "According to Charlie, the ratcatcher should have propped it open twenty minutes ago."

"Maybe he decided to shut Tiggles inside this time? Although I can't hear any yowls," said Alice.

"Sshh," said Sonny, pressing a finger to his lips.

Back along the passageway, someone was whistling a jaunty tune.

Alice cast her eyes around and pointed to another door set into the wall. Hurrying over to it, Sonny tried the handle, and it opened. A rectangular wall light buzzed in the corner, casting a soft glow over stacks of planks, ropes as thick as Alice's arms and a few pails and mops. It was one of the storage rooms Charlie had mentioned. Stepping inside, they closed the door and squeezed into a gap behind the planks.

Sonny raised his eyebrows at Alice.

Alice's mouth was dry as she heard the door to the hold rolling back.

"In you go then, Tiggles. I'll be back in an hour with a nice plate of sardines," said a voice. It was the ratcatcher.

Alice heard the cat give a meow of acknowledgement. She listened intently, but there was no sound of the door being rolled closed again, only the retreating footsteps of the ratcatcher and his echoing whistles.

"Let's go," said Sonny, walking to the storeroom door. He looked back at Alice, who was still hovering by the planks. "What's the matter?"

"There must be a reason my father's been hiding things. What if I don't like what we find in the hold?" she asked.

Sonny gave her a small smile. "I think it can be more frightening not knowing things than knowing. Come on, we'll do this together. This involves Dorothy and I'm as keen to get answers as to why she had your mother's glove as you are."

Stepping through the hold door, Alice swallowed a gasp at the sight of two rows of gleaming cars. In the half-light the vehicles seemed to be waiting in a driverless and silent traffic jam, their wheels chained to the floor as the ship ploughed across the ocean. Walking past the cars they soon reached an archway – which Alice knew from examining a plan of the ship was the entrance to luggage storage.

Stepping through the archway, Alice drew in a breath. Piles of luggage strapped into nets filled the area. Every suitcase slotted into place like a jigsaw beneath large, white-painted numbers on the inside of the hull. Looking at the keys she'd taken from her father's drawer, and hoping he wouldn't notice they were missing, Alice read the tag. "We'll find my mother's luggage in row twelve."

"But the cases and trunks are stacked above head height. How will we find it?" asked Sonny.

"If my father's coming here to look at the luggage often, it must be somewhere he can easily get to it," said Alice, winding her way through a narrow pathway between the nets.

They were almost at the prow of the ship, the hull walls narrowing to a point. The area smelled stale, of leather and dust, and the force of water on the metal outside boomed like a giant's heartbeat.

Alice swallowed back her anxiety, understanding at once why Tiggles might want the hold door propped open. Speaking of which, where was the cat?

"Look," said Sonny, who was a short way ahead and standing beneath a painted number twelve.

Catching him up, Alice saw that either side of the stacked luggage were three trunks, cardboard tags swinging from their brass handles. They were all marked *R. Townsend.*

She placed her hands on the leather, feeling every scrape, scratch and dent. A patchwork of faded labels told of long ago and far away journeys – Egypt, Brazil, Greece, Japan. She thought of her adventures scrapbook. There were so many things to learn about her mother and father, the places they had been and things they had seen, things that for some reason her father rarely spoke of.

Alice selected one of the three keys attached to the luggage tag and inserted it into the padlock on the first trunk. It didn't fit and her palms were so slick with perspiration it slipped from her fingers and skidded across the dusty floor.

"Here. Hold Rocket and let me try," said Sonny, who had again been struggling to contain the mouse in his pocket.

Alice cupped Rocket in her palms, his warmth providing a small sense of comfort as she watched Sonny retrieve the key and select a different one. The padlock mechanism turned easily and Alice's heart clattered. The leather sighed and creaked as Sonny opened the lid, as if pleased with the attention.

Sonny leaned over the trunk, his forehead creasing. "What is all of this?" he said, examining the items inside.

Alice's brain buzzed in confusion as she leaned over to look too. This was not a trunk containing clothes or personal items belonging to her mother. This contained something else that was very unusual indeed.

Chapter 25

BANK NOTES

Alice held Rocket close to her chest as she peered into her mother's trunk. It had been divided into sections by pieces of grey cardboard. Within each section sat carefully arranged files and envelopes. The trunk was a filing cabinet of sorts, and she was more curious than ever to see what it contained.

Sonny pulled out one of many envelopes stacked in the first section.

Alice could see it was very thick and addressed to her father, but the gold, embossed letters on the front showed that it was from *E. Carmichael Esq*. Even in the dim light she could see Sonny had gone quite pale. "What's the matter?" she asked.

As Sonny ran a finger over the gold lettering, she could feel his mind whirring like the beam of a lighthouse. "Elliott Carmichael. That is my grandfather's name, this is his stationery," he whispered.

"Your grandfather?" exclaimed Alice in surprise.

"Hush. Keep your voice down," said Sonny, looking around. But they were quite alone, with still no sign of Tiggles and just the creak of the hull and bumps of the suitcases knocking together for company.

"Well. Are you going to open it then?" asked Alice impatiently.

Sonny nodded. A look of puzzlement flashed across his face as he examined the contents.

"What is it?" asked Alice, as Rocket pushed his nose against her fingers.

Sonny pulled out a wad of dollar bills and waved them at her.

"Bank notes," said Alice in surprise, watching as Sonny took out the next envelope and opened it. It was also stuffed with money. "Why would your grandfather give my father this?"

Sonny shook his head limply. "I have no idea."

Rocket wriggled more forcefully, and Alice stroked his soft fur absent-mindedly, as she too puzzled over this discovery.

"There must be thousands of dollars here. Look, each envelope is dated. They go back years and years...almost twelve years," said Sonny, flicking to the very last one.

Rocket wriggled and squeaked, and Alice desperately wanted to pass him back to Sonny, but he had turned his attention to another folder containing paperwork.

"Sonny, can you take your mouse...?" Alice began, but before she could finish her sentence Rocket slipped from her fingers like butter and shimmied down her leg. "Sonny... Rocket's escaped!" she cried. She turned to see Sonny staring at a piece of paper. He was motionless, absorbed in whatever it was he was reading.

"Sonny!" said Alice again shaking his shoulder as she scanned the floor for the mouse.

Sonny jolted from his thoughts, quickly folded the paper and stuffed it into his pocket, a slow dawning horror widening his eyes. He dropped to his hands and knees and began to search the floor.

Alice felt sick. "I'm sorry. He was just so...wriggly," she said.

"It's my fault. I should have taken him back to the

cabin before we came in here," said Sonny tightly, as he felt under the nets and between the trunks.

"Look," breathed Alice.

A tortoiseshell cat sat a short way ahead of them. It licked a paw, seemingly unbothered by their presence, but then its head swivelled, and it darted away.

"No!" said Sonny, preparing to head after the cat.

The sound of footsteps and whispered voices from the vehicle hold spilled over the top of the luggage. Sonny gave Alice a desperate look. *They were no longer alone.*

Alice thought of the Blakes, a rash of goosebumps prickling her arms. Had they been followed again? But she could not allow Rocket to be caught by Tiggles. "I'll keep an eye on the cat and you find Rocket," she whispered.

Sonny nodded and Alice darted after Tiggles, her breaths shallow. She peered round the side of a large trunk in row eleven, but there was no sign of the cat. The footsteps were growing ever closer and had passed through the vehicle hold. She and Sonny were cornered. There was no escape.

Meow.

Alice looked up to see Tiggles sitting above her on a trunk. The cat gave Alice a quietly disdainful look.

Quiet shuffles and bumps came from behind, as Sonny

continued to hunt for Rocket.

"Just stay there," Alice whispered to the cat as she reached for it.

Tiggles seemed to think about her instruction, then ignored it and slunk away.

The footsteps in the hold grew nearer still. They paused every so often, as if looking for something...or someone. Alice's throat closed in fear as she thought again of the Blakes' gun and she cowered behind the luggage.

From the corner of her eye, she saw something small and silvery whiz past her shoes. Rocket! The mouse stopped for a moment, as if confused to see Alice. Seizing the opportunity, she launched herself at him, her fingers gently curving round his warm body as she landed on the ground with a heavy thump. As she lay sprawled on the dusty floor, she was dimly aware of the sound of hurrying feet. She winced as two dark shadows fell over her. She looked up in fright to see two bemused faces peering down at her.

"There you are," whispered Charlie.

"Why is Alice lying down?" whispered Miriam.

"Goodness, you gave me such a scare," said Alice, sitting up and feeling a burst of relief. "I thought you were the Blakes."

"You've found Rocket!" exclaimed Sonny, quickly

appearing by Alice's side. He gently took his pet and touched the mouse's nose with his own. Rocket wiggled his whiskers and scurried into Sonny's pocket, quite unaware of the drama he had caused.

Tiggles wound her way around Miriam's legs. "A cat... and a mouse?" she said in disbelief, looking from one to the other.

"Not the brightest idea," said Charlie, shaking his head at Sonny.

"Please don't," said Sonny weakly.

"What are you both doing down here?" asked Alice, standing up and brushing the dust from her dress.

"Miriam came looking for you again. When she told me what she'd learned I agreed we needed to find you at once. A friend said he'd cover the end of my shift and here we are," said Charlie.

Alice saw then that Miriam looked quite cross. "Charlie said you have given up on the Blakes. You do not want justice for Joseph, and you will let the ship lose the race," she said, folding her arms.

"Sonny thinks it is too dangerous to do any more, but I don't agree," said Alice, giving him a quick look.

The look Sonny gave her in return was quite peculiar. It wasn't loaded with annoyance, or disappointment at her lack of agreement, rather it was soft. "I want to stop the Blakes as much as you, but we must keep safe," he said.

Miriam gave three emphatic shakes of her head. "Doing the right thing is not easy. My papi taught science at a university. Last month some students threw stones at him. The stones cut his head. The university said because he is Jewish he cannot work there any more."

Alice saw Charlie's face contort with shock and Sonny's jaw clench.

"That's dreadful, Miriam," Alice said quietly, the reality of events in Europe coming into sharper focus again.

"Yes. And it's also very wrong," said Sonny with a frown.

"It is," said Charlie, his eyes narrowing.

Miriam shook her head. "You are kind, but I tell you this because the students who hurt Papi ran away. Mr Blake hurt Joseph and he must not be allowed to run away. The Blakes are bad people and they *must* be stopped."

A smile glimmered at the edges of Sonny's lips. "You really won't give up, will you?"

Charlie grinned. "Wait until you hear what else she has to say."

"I went to telephone booth number two at nine o'clock this morning," continued Miriam.

"Oh!" exclaimed Sonny. "I'm sorry I wasn't there."

"That is all right," said Miriam, waving a hand, clearly impatient to tell them what she had learned. "I heard Mrs Blake say they will meet R in the aft engine room at ten o'clock tonight. They will pay R and see the job is done. Afterwards they will see Peggy Thomas. Or they may see her. I do not quite understand what they said about that."

Alice grinned. Miriam was quite a different person from the cross girl they had met the previous day. Her new friend was confident, composed and had purpose. "Jolly well done, Miriam."

"Yes. Well done," said Charlie, giving her a pat on the shoulder.

The tips of Miriam's ears flushed a deep pink and her eyes sparkled with delight. "You see? We cannot give up. We can stop the Blakes now."

"Fine," said Sonny with a defeated sigh. "As long as we come up with a plan to do it safely."

"I'll swipe the crew rota from the engineer's noticeboard in the dining room," said Charlie. "That will tell us who's working in the aft engine room at ten o'clock tonight – and it should finally reveal which one of the three suspects Alice has identified is R. Then we can make a plan." He paused. "On the way, I'd like to stop off at the hospital to check on Joseph again."

"Let's all do that," said Sonny firmly.

"Yes. Good idea," Alice said, glancing at her watch. "We'd better go. The ratcatcher will be here to fetch Tiggles soon." Before closing her mother's trunk, she gave the contents a lingering look; she would have to try and come back another time.

As the four children wound their way through the luggage hold and past the stored vehicles, Alice's head was full to the brim with the things she had learned that afternoon. There seemed to be some kind of connection between her father and Sonny's grandfather, and Dorothy might be involved too. She was desperate to learn the truth, but that would have to wait as they again focused their attention on apprehending the Blakes.

Chapter 26

HOSPITAL

"I'm sorry. I can't let you in to see Joseph. He's very poorly," the nurse said to Charlie as the four children stood in the small reception area of the ship's hospital. It had that familiar aura of all hospitals, one of disinfectant and quiet.

Alice hovered in the shadows with Miriam, afraid the doctor might emerge and recognize her from the day she had helped Joseph in the swimming pool.

"Is there any change, any sign at all he'll wake up?" asked Charlie.

"I'm afraid not," said the nurse with a frown.

"But he will wake up, won't he?" persisted Charlie.

"Well…" The nurse paused and bit on her lower lip as if not knowing how much to tell them.

"Please tell us. Joseph is one of my best friends," pleaded Charlie.

"I know he is, Charlie. You're here asking about him twice a day," replied the nurse with a gentle sigh.

Charlie flushed and looked at his shoes.

"My friend hit her head. She slept for a long time. Her mami spoke with her all day and all night and then she woke up," said Miriam, stepping forward.

The nurse tilted her head. "It is said that hearing a relative's voice while unconscious can help a patient come round."

"I could bring one of the letters Joseph's received from home and read it out to him. Hearing about his family could help," suggested Charlie.

The nurse looked at Charlie as she thought. "Go on then. But be quick about it. You have fifteen minutes before the doctor returns from his break. The rest of you will have to wait here though."

Charlie grinned and hurried off to fetch the letter, while Alice, Miriam and Sonny waited outside the hospital.

Sonny was quiet – too quiet, Alice thought. She glanced

at him once or twice and caught him looking at her in a very peculiar way, as if he was just seeing her for the first time. "What's the matter?" she asked eventually.

"Nothing," he mumbled, settling Rocket in his pocket.

Alice thought about the money from Sonny's grandfather. He must be worrying about that. They badly needed answers and she saw the only way to do that would be to speak with her father and Dorothy.

"Got it," said Charlie, who had returned and was waving the letter in the air. "Wish me luck."

"Good luck," they chorused as the nurse ushered him into the ward. She turned and looked at them all. Her face softened. "Listen, you can come in too. Joseph's the only patient so you won't be disturbing anyone else."

Stepping into the ward, Alice took in the small porthole throwing a circle of light onto Joseph's bed. His face was pallid, his head bandaged.

"Hello, old friend," said Charlie, walking tentatively to the bed, as Alice, Sonny and Miriam trailed behind.

Alice couldn't believe it had only been four days since she'd seen Joseph hurrying along the dockside in Southampton. He didn't deserve to be lying here injured and alone. She felt a fresh burst of dislike for the Blakes and all they'd done and planned to do, and a fresh resolve that they *would* stop the Blakes, even if it put them in danger.

Charlie unfolded the letter and, taking a deep breath, began to read.

"Dearest Joe. It's good to hear you're still enjoying your life at sea. Your younger brothers miss you and are often found playing with the model ships you built together."

Miriam gave a sorrowful smile.

"Peter was asking the other day if he might one day work at sea too," continued Charlie. He paused and glanced at the others. "Peter is Joseph's youngest brother. He worships Joseph," he explained.

Sonny gave Alice a sidelong glance, his eyes strangely glassy. Alice thought of the matchstick model of the *Queen Mary* Joseph had built for his brother and a lump sprang to her throat.

Charlie began to speak once more, telling Joseph of a letter Peter had written to Cunard Shipping asking if he might get a job with the company, like his big brother. Cunard had written a polite letter back saying that as Peter was only ten that might be difficult.

The contents of Joseph's letter told of a warm, loving and close family who were in danger of being ripped apart by the Blakes' dreadful actions. It made Alice think about the pockets of closeness she had begun to experience with her own father and how in time that might grow. She nudged Sonny's arm and gestured for him to follow her. Standing outside the hospital once more, Alice took a deep breath, thinking of the words from Joseph's family. "What we've learned today about my father and your grandfather is confusing. But we need to put that to one side for now. I know you're anxious, but we can foil the Blakes' plan if we work together."

Sonny scuffed the toe of a shoe on the linoleum. "Together," he repeated softly. He looked up. "Yes. You're right." His hand strayed to his pocket. "Alice, I..." He paused.

"Yes?" she said.

He shook his head. "Nothing. It can wait." As Sonny turned away Alice saw him draw Rocket from his pocket and whisper something to him, as if sharing a secret with his small, furry friend.

Chapter 27

GALA DINNER

The four children sat huddled in a corner of the empty gymnasium to pore over the crew rota Charlie had swiped from the wall of the engineers' dining room. Charlie was on his lunch break and, desperate not to miss out on the investigation, had changed from his uniform and borrowed some of Sonny's smart clothes in the hope he would be able to slip around the ship unnoticed. So far it had worked.

The electric horse- and camel-riding machines, with their saddles, stirrups and reins sat unused on the black-and-white chequered floor; the caricatures of well-known sporting figures lining the walls gazing on with an air of curiosity as the four of them scrutinized the names of the engineers on duty in the aft engine room that evening.

Alice's heart jumped as she saw one familiar name. "Andrew Richardson. Junior engineer. He's one of the three people I thought we should investigate further and the only one on this rota."

"He will be in the aft engine room tonight," said Miriam.

"And his shift begins at eight o'clock," said Charlie with a frown. "Richardson's not well liked. He always pushes in the dinner queue. It's rumoured he only got a job on board because a relative works for Cunard."

Alice stood up and placed a hand on the flank of an electric horse. "It must be him. Richardson is R! We need evidence though and the only way to get that will be to catch him and the Blakes together."

"But we'd have to be in the engine room to do that," said Sonny nervously. "Please say that's not what you're thinking?"

"The Blakes must reckon they have scared me…us…off. They are banking on us keeping quiet until they've sabotaged the race and left the ship at least. They'll quite probably disappear in New York and then be jolly hard to find. We can't let that happen," said Alice.

"I can get us into the engine room," said Charlie, standing up. "The engineers use their own lift, and I know where the keys are kept. If luck's on our side, we should be able to use it unnoticed."

"And do you really believe we'll be that lucky?" asked Sonny incredulously.

"We do not wait for luck. We make our own," said Miriam firmly.

"Yes. Miriam is right. And we don't have to apprehend the Blakes ourselves, that would be foolish. But there might be a way we can get some evidence before raising the alarm," said Alice thoughtfully, as an idea crystallized in her mind.

Down every staircase, in every lift, along every passageway and past every lounge, Alice saw her father drawing admiring glances in his smart black uniform as they walked to the main dining room for the grand Gala Dinner. Passengers were dressed in their finest attire for the final night of the voyage, the array of whisper-thin lace, low-backed silk dresses and glittering jewels was quite mesmerizing. The pop of flashbulbs from the ships' photographers went off like fireworks as they rushed to record every moment.

As she walked beside her father, Alice felt like a spring on a watch that had been wound too tight. Her father was telling her facts about the ship – like that there were thirty thousand light bulbs on board, and that before the ship's maiden voyage, 15,000 people paid five shillings to come aboard for a visit and every single ashtray had been stolen as a souvenir.

Smoothing the creases from her smartest blue dress with its white collar and puffed sleeves, Alice tried to look attentive as her father spoke, but she was horribly distracted by thoughts of what she and her friends needed to do later. Would Charlie be able to borrow the engine-room lift key? Would Sonny be successful in borrowing the item she had asked him to get from his cabin? And what would the Blakes do to them if they were found out? The nagging thoughts about her own past kept bobbing up too and her head ached with it all.

The entrance to the dining room was serviced by bellboys, who were issuing polite greetings while also collecting envelopes of tips, to be shared out at the end of the voyage. The head waiter came bounding over to personally direct Alice and her father to the captain's table, but Alice found her feet glued to the carpet as she took in the huge space with its muted autumnal colours and red-upholstered dining chairs. Eight enormous pillars held up the ceiling, all of which directed the eye to a magnificent decorative wooden map of the North Atlantic on the end wall. A small crystal ship was moved along a track each day, allowing passengers to follow the *Queen Mary*'s progress as they dined.

"It's quite something, isn't it?" said Alice's father.

It really was breathtaking and under any ordinary circumstances Alice would have been planning how to do its magnificence justice as she wrote about it in her adventures scrapbook. But her eyes drifted away from her surroundings and to the passengers, scanning the tables until she saw, in the middle distance, a sight that made her breath hitch in her throat. *The Blakes.* A wine waiter had recently served them champagne and she saw them raise their glasses to one another. Her view of them disappeared as a waiter guided Alice to her seat, pulled out her chair and handed her a menu.

"The lemon sole is very good tonight, miss. Although if you would like something that's not on the menu, let me know and I will have the chef prepare it for you," said the waiter.

Alice thanked him and saw to her relief that her view of the Blakes, and their view of her, was obstructed by a wide pillar. She watched as her father greeted the lucky few passengers who had been selected to dine at the captain's table that evening. Half listening to their chatter, she noted that every other sentence seemed to be centred on how fast the ship was crossing the Atlantic and how magnificent it would be to set a new record. She curled her hands into fists on her lap.

"Alice," came a hiss to her right. She turned to see Sonny staring at her. He and Dorothy were taking their seats at a table a short distance away, both dressed smartly for the occasion with Sonny in a dark suit and Dorothy in peach chiffon. Dorothy gave Alice a quick nod of acknowledgement, then looked down at her menu. But she did not seem to be reading. She was sitting perfectly still and taking deep breaths, as if trying to calm her nerves.

"The Blakes," Alice mouthed to Sonny, gesturing in the direction of their table while Dorothy had her head down.

Sonny nodded, giving a hand signal to let her know he would keep an eye on them. He also gestured to the other side of the dining room and Alice was pleased to see Miriam being seated with her parents. Miriam would not be able to see the Blakes from where she was sitting, and Alice was glad; she wanted her friend to fully enjoy dinner with her family before they turned their attention to apprehending the couple.

"What's captured your attention?" Alice's father said, turning. He frowned and Alice saw he was looking directly at Dorothy. "Goodness. That woman with her endless questions is here."

Alice frowned.

"Don't look or she may come over," her father whispered, quickly turning away and gesturing for Alice to do the same.

But Alice continued looking for a little longer and she saw Dorothy glance up, her expression strangely blank as she stared at Alice's father. High spots of colour stained her cheeks and she looked away again and began to speak with Sonny.

Alice thought of the silk glove of her mother's that Dorothy had claimed as her own and swallowed. "What sort of questions has that woman been asking you?" she asked.

Her father placed a hand over his glass, signalling to the wine waiter he did not want a drink. "She's pleasant enough but rather peculiar, very keen to know about my career and how I've risen through the ranks. Asked a lot of questions about you, too, when she found out I had a daughter."

Alice turned this new information over in her mind, remembering Dorothy's strange behaviour towards her when they'd first met. Then there was her help in getting Alice out of the isolation ward, followed by the sudden announcement that she and Sonny were leaving the ship. These thoughts were interrupted by a man with bulbous eyes taking a seat to her right. The gold stripes on his lapels gleamed in the overhead lights.

"Mr Lewis, this is Alice, my daughter. Alice, this is the chief engineer," said Alice's father leaning forward to make the introductions.

Alice took a sip of iced water to try and melt the lump in her throat. *The chief engineer.* The evening was getting more difficult by the second.

Mr Lewis smiled. "Very pleased to meet you, Alice. I hope you've enjoyed the voyage?"

"Oh yes, very much, thank you," she said.

"It's been a very uncomplicated run across the Atlantic; nice and smooth," he said, pouring himself a glass of water.

Alice smiled faintly. If only he knew the truth.

"I suppose your nephew and the rest of the team have been working hard on that?" said Alice's father with a smile. "The captain commended my decision to push on through the fog and has placed a call to Cunard back in

Southampton to say we're on track to win the race."

Mr Lewis took a sip of his drink. "Excellent news. Anyway, shall we order? I mustn't leave the boilers for too long. One of them was playing up today."

"Oh?" said Alice, her ears pricking up.

Mr Lewis laughed. "Nothing to worry about. It's cranked up the heat down in the engine room though. Poor men are sweating buckets down there."

"How hot is it?" asked Alice, swallowing her unease.

"Hot enough for them to need special shoes or else their soles would melt," said the chief engineer with a grimace.

"The engineers work four-hour shifts because of the heat. It really is extreme," added Alice's father, as he buttered a bread roll.

Alice sat back in her seat and felt a deep dismay as the waiter took their orders. How would she and Sonny cope in the heat? She had to make sure Rocket did not come with them; he was far too delicate and would not survive.

The noise levels in the dining room were rising and Alice's father was now occupied by the dinner guest to his left, explaining how changes in speed were issued from the wheelhouse to the engine room and that both places needed to be synchronized for the ship to run effectively. Alice saw with dismay there would be no opportunity to question him further on Dorothy, the things she had learned from the baroness and the money that she and Sonny had discovered in the hold.

An endless stream of delicious dishes began to arrive at the table and Alice was surprised to find that all the worrying meant she had a tremendous appetite for the cream of mushroom soup, fillet of lemon sole and chocolate-and-vanilla ice cream and wafers she found placed in front of her.

Her father was animated throughout the meal, talking to each passenger in turn and patiently answering their questions. But she could tell from the way his knee kept jiggling and accidentally bumping into hers that he was keen to leave.

"I think we can go now," he eventually whispered to Alice, as she scooped up the last of her ice cream.

"Staff Captain Townsend. I don't think we've been introduced," said a voice over Alice's right shoulder.

It was a cold and calculating voice that sent Alice's dessertspoon clattering into her dish. She slowly looked up to see Mr Blake leering over the table, his wife standing by his side with a sickly smile plastered over her tight cheeks.

Alice gripped her knees and sat up straighter.

"Good evening. I hope you've enjoyed the voyage, Mr and Mrs..." her father said, pushing back his chair and holding out a hand to greet them.

"The name's Blake," said Mr Blake in his cool tone. "My wife and I have very much enjoyed the voyage. Well done on setting a new Atlantic crossing record. Quite an achievement."

Alice gripped her knees harder. From the corner of her eye, she saw Mrs Blake's fingers tighten around her black handbag. It was the perfect size in which to conceal a small gun.

"We haven't quite done it yet, but with luck on our side I think the *Queen Mary* is in with a good chance of winning the trophy," her father replied with a smile. "Speaking of which, I really must return to my duties in the wheelhouse. I'm sure my daughter is keen to get back to her reading and embroidery too."

"Of course," said Mrs Blake smoothly, looking at Alice. "They sound like very worthy pursuits for a young lady. And we wouldn't want anything to...obstruct either of your evenings."

Alice's shoulders stiffened. She saw her father give the Blakes a slightly puzzled look, then he gestured for Alice to stand up and follow him.

Alice felt unsteady, as if the ship was now navigating a violent storm. Gratefully taking the arm her father offered, they wound their way out of the room. At the doors she turned to look back. The Blakes were following a short way behind, smirks grazing their lips. Behind them she saw Sonny, his jaw clenched and his eyes like thunder as he watched them too. He gave Alice the briefest of nods. She felt a white-hot rage rattle through her, deciding that whatever it took tonight they *would* stop the Blakes.

Chapter 28

ENGINE ROOM

It was just before nine-thirty in the evening and Alice could feel heat beginning to rise through the floor of the engineers' lift as it clunked its way down to the engine room.

"I can't believe the Blakes were bold enough to speak with your father like that at dinner," said Charlie, shaking his head as he operated the lift. Just as planned, he'd taken the spare key from the key pound when his shift had ended, temporarily replacing it with his own in the hope he'd able to swap them back before anyone noticed.

"The Blakes are rotten through and through all right,"

said Alice, tucking her thin blouse into her navy slacks. After speaking with the chief engineer, she had suggested they all wear their lightest clothes to keep them cool in the belly of the ship.

Pearl had arrived with fresh towels just as Alice had finished changing and had given her a questioning look. "Off out again?"

Alice had simply nodded.

Pearl had placed the towels down and folded her arms. "I don't know what this mystery of yours is, but be careful. If your father comes back and you're not here...well, I'd hate to see you get into trouble."

Alice had given Pearl a quick nod and finished tying up her plimsolls, knowing it was already too late for that. Her father was bound to find out what they had done, but if they successfully exposed the Blakes, she would accept his punishment without complaint.

She glanced at the rubber soles of her plimsolls now, hoping they would stand up to the extreme heat of the engine room.

Sonny gave Alice a sidelong glance. It was a strange and almost secretive look and she wondered what he was thinking. He cleared his throat and pulled Dorothy's camera from his trouser pocket. "I hope your idea works."

"Me too," said Alice. She had asked Sonny to borrow the camera thinking there might be enough light in the engine room to capture a photograph of the Blakes handing over the payment to Andrew Richardson. Once they had this evidence, it was just the small matter of somehow raising the alarm before Richardson had a chance to slow the ship down. "You're sure Rocket is safe and sound in your cabin?" she asked him.

Sonny nodded. "I'm quite sure. I fixed the door of his cage with some pipe cleaners I borrowed from the children's playroom."

"Good. I like your mouse," said Miriam. "Maybe I will get one in America."

Alice felt a burst of warmth for her new friends. The circumstances that had thrown them together had brought a closeness she would miss once Sonny and Miriam disembarked the following day.

"The Blakes will most likely use the crew stairs to access the aft engine room to deliver the payment to Richardson and check he follows their instructions," said Charlie as the lift moved ever downwards.

"But they will be seen," said Miriam with a frown.

"Richardson must be helping them," said Alice. She had spent a while studying a cross-section drawing of the ship that she'd stuck in her adventures scrapbook to help plan their route, but it was a picture and didn't have all the detail she needed.

"You shouldn't have any trouble locating Richardson. He's tall and has a moustache that looks a like a dead rat," said Charlie. He paused and looked at Sonny. "Maybe it's better if I go with Alice instead?"

"No," said Sonny quickly, almost too quickly. He took a breath. "We agreed it's safer to split up. Anyway, you know how to operate the lift. We may need help making a quick exit."

A sudden loud whomp caused Sonny, Miriam and Alice to exchange anxious glances.

"What was that?" Miriam whispered.

"It's the force of the ocean against the ship's hull. We're below the waterline now," said Charlie calmly. But the tapping of his fingers on his trouser legs gave away his nerves.

Alice pressed her back against the wall of the lift, trying not to think of the water surrounding them.

"Don't worry. I've been on this ship for months and there hasn't been a single leak," whispered Sonny.

"Well, except during that storm in April when..." began Charlie. He was met with a chorus of quiet groans and shaking heads, and he raised a hand in apology. "Sorry," he said meekly.

Alice wiped at the beads of sweat gathering in her hairline and tightened her ponytail. The air was becoming stifling.

Sonny checked the camera buttons were in working order.

Miriam crossed her arms, then uncrossed them again, unable to keep still.

Clunk.

The lift came to a stop, depositing them in the giant underbelly of the ship. The doors drew back and a whoosh of furnace-hot air rushed in to greet them. It whisked Alice's breath from her lungs and in the space of seconds their faces all had a rosy glow.

Miriam reached forward and gave Alice a quick hug. "Good luck," she whispered.

Alice felt Sonny slip past her, and she made to follow him. "Good luck to you too. We'll be back as soon as we can, hopefully with pictures on the camera that will prove Richardson and the Blakes are in this together. Then we'll raise the alarm."

Charlie gave a nod and pressed a button on the lift control panel. His and Miriam's concerned faces disappeared as the doors slid closed.

Alice and Sonny were at the very heart of the ship where, upon every turn of the ship's four propellors, the water they drank and electricity they used was produced and controlled. Thumps, groans, clunks, clicks, whirrs, and bursts of steam filled the cavernous space that arched upwards like a giant hangar. Pipes of all shapes and sizes held together by metal bands crossed the ceiling and walls, as heat rose from the metal walkway like a fire had been lit beneath them.

"This is...too hot," said Sonny, leaning into Alice's ear. With the surrounding noise they would need to shout to get one another's attention.

"We'll be as quick as we can," replied Alice.

To their left and right, huge metal watertight doors were firmly closed. The door to the left led to the back of the ship, meaning they had to pass through it to get to the aft engine room.

Alice set off across the metal walkway, heat pulsing through the soles of her shoes. She tucked her bare arms to her sides, keeping them well away from pipes dripping with condensation.

"How do we get through the watertight door?" asked Sonny.

"We pull that lever, I think," said Alice, pointing to the controls on the wall beside the door.

"But there's no window. How will we know if anyone is on the other side?" asked Sonny.

Alice swallowed. "We won't know until it opens."

Sonny took a deep breath, then stepped over and placed a hand on the rubber-coated lever. "Ready?" he said, his jaw clenching.

"Ready," Alice replied, watching and waiting as her friend slid the lever down. A small light above the controls shone green and, with a clunk, the door began to roll back.

Chapter 29

FULL STEAM AHEAD

The watertight door rolled back quickly and efficiently, and Alice felt a surge of relief on finding that she and Sonny were still alone in this part of the ship's engine room. She stepped over the threshold and paused, quietly watching as Sonny used a second lever to close the door behind them.

The walkway they now found themselves on was also constructed of metal grating, but through its diamond-patterned holes Alice realized that another working area lay beneath them. With a burst of alarm, she saw that just below their feet two men in overalls were deep in conversation. Seeing that neither man had a moustache and so could not be Richardson, she cowered against the door, gesturing for Sonny to do the same.

Sonny stood back and wiped his forehead on his shirtsleeve. His face was beetroot red, and his eyes puffy.

Keeping her eyes glued to the grating, Alice watched the two men move out of sight.

Sonny closed his eyes and sucked in long, deep breaths.

Alice touched him on the arm and his eyes flicked open. "Are you all right?" she asked.

Sonny placed a hand on his chest. "So hot…hard to breathe," he said, his face strained with the exertion of speaking.

Alice felt her anxiety increase like the pressure inside one of the ship's boilers. Sonny was looking quite unwell. She threw a quick glance at her watch. The Blakes were due to make an appearance in around fifteen minutes. Would either of them be able to stand the heat for that long? Peering into the distance, Alice saw what looked like the edge of a large control panel. This had to be the place where the Blakes were meeting Richardson to hand over the payment.

Alice reached for Sonny's hand. "Come on," she said.

Sonny looked down at Alice's hand. His eyes were

watery, as if he might cry. He opened his mouth to say something, then closed it again.

Alice felt a pinch at the base of her throat. "It is devilishly hot in here, but all we need is one photograph of the Blakes and Richardson, then we can go."

Sonny nodded and jammed his sweaty palm against hers.

The children crept across the metal grating, Alice scanning the area below and ahead for any sign of life. Reaching the end of the walkway, they now had a clear view of the control panel. A bewildering array of large and small round dials, switches and levers covered a metal wall the size of a small house. In front of the panel, staring at them like a large black-and-bronze eye, was the engine room telegraph which set the ship's speed. It was currently locked at *Full steam ahead.*

Sonny let out a wheezy cough and Alice saw his cheeks were even redder than before, his skin now mottled. He was reacting very badly to the heat indeed. The weight of his hand was dragging her down and she was suddenly afraid he might collapse. She had to find a place for him to sit and recover.

To the right of the control panel stood a thick white pipe as high as Alice's waist. Steering Sonny over to the pipe, she helped him crouch behind it. He gave her an apologetic look. "It's this heat...my chest..." he gasped. "I'm sorry. I...I should be looking after you."

Alice rested a hand on one of his knees. "We look after each other down here. Don't speak. Just breathe." She watched him for a few seconds as his chest heaved with the effort of taking in the overheated air. Her stomach turned. Sonny was far more important than the Blakes. "I need to get you back to the lift," she said.

Sonny held his head in his hands. "No. We...must stop... the Blakes. For...Joseph...and your father," he said haltingly.

"But you're not well," protested Alice.

"No," barked Sonny, more vehemently this time. He looked up, the muscles in his jaw twitching and Alice knew his decision was final.

Alice tried to clamp down her rising anxiety. They had badly underestimated the conditions down here. She pushed a hand into her pocket searching for a handkerchief to wipe her sweaty face and felt a small packet nestling there. It was the lemon sherbets Pearl had given her. Prising the warm sticky sweets apart, Alice thought of Pearl's bravery as she survived the sinking of the *Titanic* and passed a molten sweet to Sonny. "Here, take this. It may help."

Sonny popped the sweet into his mouth and closed his eyes.

A series of loud clicks made Alice turn and peep over the top of the pipe. A man with a fat moustache wearing blue overalls and black gloves was now standing by the control panel. That had to be Richardson. She saw him look at his watch, then walk to a metal door set into the wall a short distance away. Pulling a key from his pocket, he glanced around, then unlocked the door and opened it.

Alice's shoulders stiffened and she drew in a breath as the Blakes entered the engine room. Mrs Blake held a small brown package and Mr Blake's face was steely, his hands lodged in his trouser pockets as he stood beside his wife.

Alice slid back down behind the pipe. "You'll need to give me the camera," she said.

"No...I can do it," said Sonny thinly, struggling to turn round. He slipped and placed a hand on the hot metal floor to steady himself. His face contorted in pain. Alice winced. Shaking his head in annoyance, Sonny passed the camera to Alice.

Peering over the top of the pipe once more, Alice's pulse thundered in her ears, louder than any of the surrounding machinery. The Blakes were now talking with Richardson, but it was too noisy to hear what was being said.

Mrs Blake held out the package to Richardson.

Alice lifted the camera and clicked, her fingers slick with perspiration. She wound the film and clicked again as Richardson took the package and placed it in his overall pocket. The Blakes must be handing over the gold. She did the same again as Richardson shook hands with Mr Blake, and then Mrs Blake.

The shrill ring of a telephone on the control panel made Richardson turn. Alice followed his gaze and saw that stamped above the telephone was one word. *Wheelhouse.* The call must be an instruction coming down from the captain, or her father.

Richardson gestured at the ringing telephone and made a throat cutting gesture with one hand. He laughed, his rat-like moustache dancing unpleasantly against his cheeks.

The Blakes smiled; curling, supercilious smiles that made Alice feel like her veins were flowing hot with rage. Richardson was going to ignore the instruction coming from the wheelhouse.

She saw the Blakes looking at the telegraph and Alice looked at it too. Suddenly, she understood why the Blakes were so delighted. The clicks she had heard while hiding behind the pipe must have been the sound of Richardson pulling the telegraph lever to *Half ahead*. This would send a signal to the engineers working on the boilers that the ship should be slowed down! The wheelhouse must have registered this and were calling to see what was happening.

Alice glanced at Sonny. His head was still in his hands as he sucked on the lemon sherbet, but his breathing seemed a little easier. Carefully placing the camera in his lap, she turned her attention back to the Blakes and Richardson.

The Blakes were walking back to the door in the wall, and Richardson was following them. The telephone was still ringing and ringing. Why were none of the other engineers coming to investigate? Alice gritted her teeth. The engineers might already be reducing the ship's speed and it could take a while to increase it again. She could not let this ship lose the Blue Riband race. Lurching from her hiding place she ran to the telegraph and made a grab for the lever.

"Hey!" yelled a voice.

Alice spun around and saw Richardson gawping at her.

Mr Blake gave Alice a look which made her shrink inside. His lips curled into a snarl and he reached into his pocket. He had whipped out a gun and was pointing it directly at her.

Chapter 30

CHIEF ENGINEER

Mr Blake's eyes were narrowed and focused as he pointed the gun at Alice. She blinked, thinking of her father in the wheelhouse and the telephone still clanging its urgent ring behind her. The revolutions of the steam turbines and propellors would soon be decreasing and the ship losing speed. There was nothing to be done. Sonny was at least safe for now, hidden behind the pipe, but she was too afraid to move, too afraid to do anything at all.

"Over here," shouted someone from the far end of the walkway. Alice swallowed a gasp. It was Miriam, and Charlie was close behind her!

Miriam's eyes flashed with intent as she stood looking at the Blakes.

Mr Blake swung round, the gun now pointing at Miriam, who, rather than looking shocked, looked furious.

"Put that down," she yelled, striding towards him. "You are a bad, bad, man."

"No, Miriam," shouted Charlie, trying to restrain her, but Miriam charged towards Mr Blake, who stood looking at her in bewilderment.

"Do something," Mrs Blake cried.

Mr Blake snapped out of his trance and his fingers tightened round the gun.

"No!" Alice yelled, darting forward in a bid to protect her friends. As the words left her lips, something flew over her head, hitting Mr Blake square between the shoulder blades. He jolted forward and the gun fell from his hands, clattering through a gap at the edge of the grating to the area below.

Mr Blake swung back to look at Alice, his face looking as if it was about to pop like an overripe raspberry. At his feet lay Dorothy's camera. Alice briefly turned and saw Sonny standing behind the pipe, his arm still outstretched. He had thrown the camera as a distraction to help them.

"How dare you," yelled Mrs Blake, picking up the

camera. Her eyes were ovals of white-hot fury. "You've been taking pictures of us!"

Charlie and Miriam were now bravely marching along the walkway, shoulder to shoulder.

Alice felt a hand on her arm. It was Sonny. He jabbed a finger at the ship's telegraph and Alice gave him a quick nod of understanding. Grasping the hot lever, she heaved it towards her until it could go no further. *Full steam ahead.*

A few moments later the telephone on the control panel stopped ringing.

Richardson looked stricken and confused by what was happening. He tapped Mr Blake on the shoulder and made an urgent gesture at the door they had come through. They began to hurry towards it.

"They're going to escape," croaked Alice, her throat as dry as coal dust.

"Must...stop them," wheezed Sonny angrily.

"What's going on in here?" The shout came from a furious-looking man with bulbous eyes, rushing up the stairs from the working area below. The stripes on his lapels glinted in the low light. Alice recognized him at once. It was Mr Lewis, the chief engineer she had met at dinner that evening.

In the commotion, Richardson slipped through the

now-open door, gesturing for the Blakes to do the same.

Mrs Blake balled her hands into fists and scowled. Mr Blake threw the children a look that could have chilled the overheated air. The three of them disappeared and the door slammed shut.

"No!" exclaimed Alice, ignoring Mr Lewis and running to the door. She heard Sonny close behind and the sounds of Charlie and Miriam approaching. She tugged on the door handle, her fingers recoiling from the heat. It wouldn't open. She tugged it again. *They had locked the door from the other side.*

She turned to Sonny. "They've gone," she said limply, as Mr Lewis marched towards them.

Sonny's jaw twitched and he pulled on the door handle himself.

"There must be a way to stop them," said Charlie, banging on the door in frustration.

"It must not end like this," cried Miriam.

"Children? In my engine room!" yelled Mr Lewis.

The four children turned in tandem to see his thunderous face.

Alice pointed to the door. "The Blakes...Richardson... they are..."

Mr Lewis's eyes narrowed. "Miss Townsend?" he

interrupted, his voice rising several octaves. "What in heaven's name…?" He shook his head so hard Alice wondered if it would fall off. "It's far too dangerous for you to be down here. It's breaking every rule and regulation in the book. In all my days at sea I've never known anything like this."

Alice looked through the metal grating and caught a glimpse of the gun. She pointed. "There's a…"

"Stop! Don't say another word," Mr Lewis bellowed, his eyes darting from the gun to the door Richardson and the Blakes had vanished through.

"But two passengers working for Diamond Shipping tried to slow the *Queen Mary* so it would lose the Blue Riband race. They paid an engineer called Richardson to make that happen. They escaped through that door and must be stopped," said Alice, willing him to listen and take action.

Mr Lewis's lips pressed together into a paper-thin line.

Charlie stepped forward and bravely looked Mr Lewis in the eye. "Joseph Wilks – a steward on board – was deliberately injured because he wouldn't help these passengers with their plan to sabotage the ship. They're bad people and had that gun down there…"

"Stop. Speaking," bellowed Mr Lewis, holding up a hand

as if he was a policeman stopping traffic. His eyes seemed to pop out of his head even further as he regarded each of the children in turn. "I'm taking you to the engineers' mess room while I inform the staff captain of this. He will be very unhappy."

Alice felt this to be a huge understatement. Her father would be furious! Her friends' heads were low, feeling the same sense of defeat as she was. They had stopped the ship from being slowed down for now, but the Blakes had got away – along with the camera and proof of their attempted crime – and now it was the four of them who seemed to be in trouble. Things were looking very bad for them all indeed.

Chapter 31

PEGGY THOMAS

After taking the children up in the lift and locking them in the engineers' mess room on Sun Deck, Mr Lewis's footsteps could be heard hurrying away, leaving Alice, Sonny, Miriam and Charlie alone. Sonny strode to the sink and drank noisily from the tap as Charlie stood by the door.

"You didn't wait in the lift. You came to help us," Alice said to Miriam.

"We could not let you face the Blakes and Richardson alone," said Miriam firmly.

"Miriam was worried. She insisted we came to see if you

needed help. It's a good job we did," said Charlie.

"You were so brave, Miriam, standing up to Mr Blake like that," said Alice, hugging her friend tight.

"You were all brave," said Sonny, wiping his mouth on his shirtsleeve. "I can't believe Mr Blake pointed the gun at you all."

"That was frightening," admitted Alice, a shiver skittering across her shoulders at the memory. "Thank you for throwing the camera, Sonny. I know it means we lost the evidence, but...well...you saved me...and all of us really."

Sonny's cheeks pinked. "I'm just glad there was something I could do in the end. Sorry for being so hopeless down there."

Alice gave him a soft smile and sank into a chair. "I'm just glad you're all right now. At least Mr Lewis retrieved the gun. He said he would look into it."

"Mr Lewis was cross, but he didn't have much to say about it all," said Charlie with a frown, his ear now pressed to the door.

Miriam perched on a chair beside Alice. "I do not think Mr Lewis was listening to us. But why not?"

They sat in silence for a while, the vibrations of the ship shuddering through the floor.

"I suppose it's embarrassing, one of his own engineers embroiled in a plot to slow the ship," said Sonny, the puffiness in his cheeks now receding thanks to the cooler air. "And grown-ups often have trouble listening to children."

"Why didn't Mr Lewis take us to my father and tell him what happened?" pondered Alice, thinking it a little odd that they had been locked up and not handed over straight away.

"Alice. Can I have a quiet word?" asked Sonny. He was looking at her with the same peculiar expression he'd had after their visit to the hold earlier that day.

Alice nodded and stood up.

Sonny swallowed. He looked nervous as he steered her to the corner of the room. "I need to tell you..."

"Quiet. It sounds like Mr Lewis is coming back – and he's got someone with him," hissed Charlie, his ear still to the door.

Alice's stomach dropped. Had he returned with her father? There was the sound of a door closing then muffled voices, but they weren't coming from outside the mess room. She glanced round, her eyes settling on a ventilation grate in the wall. "Look," she said, pointing.

"The voices are coming from the room next door,"

whispered Charlie, hurrying to the vent and crouching down.

Alice joined him, straining to hear the conversation.

"You fool, Andrew," Alice heard Mr Lewis say curtly. "The Blakes bringing a gun on board was a mistake."

"I swear I knew nothing about it, Uncle," replied a whiny voice. It was Richardson!

Charlie raised his eyebrows and nudged Alice. She suddenly remembered what he'd said about Richardson having a relative who also worked for Cunard, and her father mentioning the chief engineer's nephew when they were at dinner. The chief engineer was Richardson's uncle!

"I've put the gun in my safe and will chuck it overboard later. You told me the Blakes had warned those children to stop their meddling," said Mr Lewis.

Alice exchanged a horrified look with Charlie. Mr Lewis and Richardson had both been helping the Blakes. She felt a burst of hot indignation and beckoned Sonny and Miriam over to listen.

"At least the Blakes paid us in full, after recovering the gold those children took," said Richardson.

Charlie tutted, his cheeks reddening.

Miriam placed a hand on his arm and shushed him.

"Where are the Blakes now?" asked Mr Lewis.

"After the children messed up our plan to reduce the

ship's speed, the Blakes signalled their support vessel, *Peggy Thomas*. She's about half a mile off the *Queen Mary*'s stern. They'll be picked up from the water after jumping port-side from Capstan Deck."

"*Peggy Thomas* is a boat," whispered Sonny, his cheeks tightening.

Alice's head was spinning. Peggy wasn't a person, but the vessel the Blakes were planning to escape in. She remembered the diving suits in their suitcase, and Mrs Blake ploughing up and down in the pool the day they hunted for the package. Going overboard must have been their backup plan in case things went wrong, which they clearly had now.

"They'll risk their lives doing that," said Mr Lewis in a low voice.

"The head baker on the *Titanic* survived the waters of the North Atlantic for two hours after the ship sank. The Blakes will only be in the water for a short while and they've planned their escape well," insisted Richardson.

There was a short pause. "I suppose it would be more dangerous for them to stay on board. Those children know Mr Blake tried to silence Joseph Wilks. That was another mistake the Blakes made in this whole, sorry mess. I wish you'd never suggested we help them," said Mr Lewis.

"But you agreed the payment was too good to turn down," whined Richardson. "Anyway, what'll we do about the children? As soon as you let them out, they'll report me."

"Children lie all the time. They have no proof. If we deny their accusations, we should come out of this all right," said Mr Lewis grimly.

"They are perfectly dreadful," whispered Alice, and Miriam gave a fierce nod of agreement.

"Bring me the gold tomorrow. I'll cash it in at a bank when we get to New York. After all our efforts we deserve to be paid, even though the plan failed. Right, I must get back to the engine room. I've got to explain to the captain why the speed dropped to *Half ahead* for a short while. I told him earlier one of the boilers had been playing up and he should accept that as an excuse. I'll keep the children up here a bit longer to give the Blakes a chance to get away. I suggest you get off to bed and we both deny knowing the Blakes if we're asked. Do you understand?" said Mr Lewis.

There was the sound of a door opening and closing and two sets of footsteps walking away. The heavy door leading to the deck banged closed. They were alone again.

"How rotten and selfish," said Alice, folding her arms across her stomach. "They've both been in on the plan all along and are going to let the Blakes escape on their boat."

For some reason Charlie didn't seem as bothered by this news as Alice thought he might. "I reckon it's safe for us to leave," he said, pressing his ear to the door again.

"What do you mean? We're locked in!" blustered Sonny, plonking his hands on his hips.

Alice felt a pang of regret at how badly things had gone wrong.

"Well...not for much longer," said Charlie, slipping a hand into his pocket.

"What do you mean?" huffed Miriam impatiently.

"Ta-da," Charlie said with a grin, holding something small and shiny in the air. He bowed, as if he had just performed a specular magic trick and was waiting for the audience's applause.

Alice blinked. "Is that what I think it is?"

"A master door key," said Sonny, his cheeks cracking into a smile.

"When...? How...?" stuttered Miriam.

Charlie grinned. "Being around you lot and trying to solve this mystery made me see it pays to think ahead. When I took the engineers' lift key, I took the opportunity of borrowing their master key too."

"Well done," said Alice, patting him on the back.

Miriam reached up and flung her arms round Charlie's neck and his ears pinked at the tips.

Charlie unlocked the door and peered into the passageway. Beckoning them forward, they crept past Mr Lewis's office and out onto the deck.

The inky sky was studded with stars and in the distance the sound of a jazz band could be heard.

Alice felt a fresh stab of anger at everything the Blakes, Mr Lewis and Richardson had done, darkness swelling inside her like a balloon. Joseph was hurt and in hospital, his loving family desperate for news. The Blakes had attempted to slow the ship and cheat it out of winning a much-deserved trophy, and her father out of his promotion. She recalled the fear she had felt when Mr Blake had pointed his gun at her and her friends and channelled it into a fresh determination to make him and his accomplices account for their actions.

"What now?" asked Miriam.

Alice gritted her teeth. There really was only one thing to do. "The Blakes could be escaping at this very moment. We must stop them at once."

Chapter 32

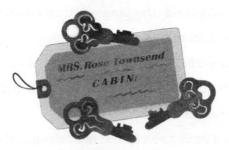

ESCAPE

The four children hurried to the stern of the ship and Capstan Deck, from where Richardson had said the Blakes would escape.

"Look! That could be the *Peggy Thomas*," said Alice. A pinprick of light flashed to the east, some distance away. It flashed again.

The door to the Verandah Grill opened, and the high notes of a saxophone spiralled into the night. A group of passengers tumbled out, guffawing with laughter, oblivious to the children and their quest.

Alice pushed on, heading past a low-slung sports net and down some steps.

"Wait," said Sonny, tugging on Alice's sleeve. "You're rushing in without thinking this through."

Alice paused and looked back at her friends.

"Sonny's right," admitted Charlie. "We must tell someone what's happened."

Logic told Alice this was the right thing to do, but she also feared time would be wasted. If the Blakes escaped overboard it would leave them with no evidence and no justice for Joseph. It would be their word against the chief engineer's.

"We must get help, Alice," said Miriam firmly.

Alice curled her fingers round the handrail. While part of her was still tempted to dash on and try and stop the Blakes, perhaps it was wiser to listen. "Fine. We'll separate again – two of us will keep an eye on the Blakes until help arrives and two go to the wheelhouse to raise the alarm."

"I'm staying with you," Sonny said to Alice firmly, moving to stand by her side.

"Miriam and I will go to the wheelhouse then," said Charlie, looking at Miriam, who gave a firm nod of agreement.

"Make sure Alice's father knows what's happened. Tell

him…tell him Alice is safe with Hudson," said Sonny, his face drawn in the moonlight.

"Hudson?" asked Charlie with a frown.

"Yes, that's my full name," replied Sonny, steering Alice down the steps.

Alice glanced at her friend as they made their way down. "You don't have to keep me safe; I can look after myself."

"Shhh. I can hear something," said Sonny, ignoring Alice and crouching to peer through the gaps in the railings.

Alice dropped down beside him, her eyes scanning over the large vertical drums and winding equipment throwing monstrous shadows onto Capstan Deck. It was a working part of the ship and open to third-class passengers, who sat out on a pleasant day, but no one visited at night. It would provide the perfect hiding place for the Blakes. She heard a peculiar sucking noise coming from below.

"There's that sound again," whispered Sonny with a frown.

"Ouch. No. You put it on like this," said a low voice from behind a large grey winding machine. It was Mr Blake.

"Are you sure these suits will keep us warm in the water while we wait to be picked up?" said Mrs Blake, her voice thin.

"They were expensive, so I jolly well hope so," replied Mr Blake curtly.

The lights of the *Peggy Thomas* blinked; the vessel was moving closer. It sounded as if the Blakes were almost ready to launch themselves overboard. It was a foolhardy and desperate plan, and despite Alice's keen dislike for them, she worried Mr Lewis was right, and it would prove fatal. "We've got to delay them," she whispered.

Sonny's eyes widened. "What? No, Alice! We must wait for help to arrive."

Ignoring the alarm in her friend's eyes, Alice climbed over the locked gate separating the first- and third-class areas of deck and started off once more down a final narrow set of steps to Capstan Deck. Tucking herself behind a vertical black-and-white drum, she saw the Blakes were shimmying into black rubber diving suits. By their feet lay two of the *Queen Mary*'s bulky lifebelts. They would need those to stay afloat until the *Peggy Thomas* rescued them.

The Blakes had their backs to Alice and were fully absorbed in adjusting their suits. Before she had time to fully think through her plan, Alice darted across to one of the lifebelts, picked it up and ran back behind the drum, her heart hammering. Without the safety of a lifebelt, surely they would not risk going overboard.

"What have you done with my lifebelt?" said Mr Blake a few moments later, puzzlement straining his voice.

There was a short pause. "It was here a moment ago," said Mrs Blake.

Alice's stomach clenched with anxiety as she cowered behind the drum, listening to the scuffles and scrapes as they searched for it. She glanced up to where she had left Sonny, hoping help was on its way, but the only sounds were the wind, the vibrations of the ship and the surge of the wake from its giant propellors.

"The belt can't have jolly well moved on its own," snapped Mr Blake.

"Freddie, we have company," said Mrs Blake.

Alice looked up to see Mrs Blake's pale face peering over the top of the drum. Whispers of hair escaped from her swimming cap, dancing like snakes in the gusty breeze. Alice locked her arms round the lifebelt, determined not to let it go despite her fear. "We've raised the alarm. My father will be here any minute to stop you," she said, fighting the tremor in her throat.

Mrs Blake yanked the lifebelt from Alice's arms, causing her to sit down with a heavy thump. "Your father? He's the reason we are in this mess," she spat.

Alice felt a wave of dizziness as she sat looking up at Mrs Blake. What had her father got to do with the Blakes?

Mr Blake stepped over, his eyes widening at the sight of Alice sitting on the deck. At the same time, she became aware of the thud of feet on the wooden steps behind her.

"Don't you dare hurt her," said Sonny, appearing by her side. His eyes flashed as he faced the Blakes.

Alice stood up and sidled close to her friend, relieved she was no longer alone.

"How nice to see you again, Hudson," said Mrs Blake with a smirk. "I must say, though, I am annoyed at you and your friends' meddling. Your grandfather would not have approved at all."

Alice blinked. She glanced at Sonny uncertainly. "You… you know the Blakes?"

"No," said Sonny, taking a step back. "I…I'd never seen them before this voyage."

Mr Blake threw them both a look of irritation as he helped his wife into her lifebelt, quickly tying the straps around her waist.

"You might not remember me, but I remember you," said Mrs Blake, her eyes glinting with mischief. "My husband and I worked for your grandfather for years. We were his trusted confidants and knew all his secrets.

Anything he asked for, we made happen."

"Cora, that's enough," said Mr Blake, giving her an anxious glance as he began to put on his own lifebelt.

Cora Blake ignored her husband and continued to look at Sonny quite triumphantly. "We met you a few years ago, shortly after your grandfather bought the Diamond Shipping Company."

Alice drew in a sharp breath at this new information. Sonny's grandfather had owned Diamond Shipping! That meant he owned the *Sapphire*, the current holder of the Blue Riband trophy. The threads binding her and Sonny joined, then snapped as she fought to understand the truth.

Mr Blake left his wife and ran to the railing to peer over the side of the ship, doing up the ties of his lifebelt on the way.

"My grandfather owned...Diamond Shipping?" stuttered Sonny. He looked limp, like a wrung-out cloth.

Mrs Blake gave both Alice and Sonny an arrow-like glare. "He was grandfather to both of you, of course."

Alice's shoulders tensed. *What could she mean?* The fizz of sea spray, the sound of Mr Blake urging his wife to hurry, Sonny's guttural intake of breath; she was dimly aware of all those things as she grappled to understand the meaning behind Mrs Blake's words. Sonny's grandfather had sent her father wads of bank notes for many years before he died. Her mother's glove had been found in Sonny's cabin. Then there was Dorothy's strange behaviour. Was this the answer she had been looking for? *Could she and Sonny be related?*

Cora Blake's eyes widened as she peered at Alice. "Wait. You're looking quite shocked. Don't you know any of this?"

Alice turned to Sonny. He was perhaps not as overwhelmed by this news as she would have expected, but his jaw moved as he ground his teeth.

"He's my grandfather too?" Alice croaked. The question felt like thin ice at the edge of a pond, and she desperately wanted to move away from that edge.

"I was going to tell you," Sonny said softly. "I started to piece it all together when we looked in the trunk today." He was giving Alice an open look which made her see this was the truth.

In an instant her world had shifted and would never be the same. Alice wrapped her arms round her middle and tried to quell her shivers.

Cora Blake was looking at them with amusement, as if they were a sideshow in a circus.

Mr Blake was peering over the stern to the lights of the

Peggy Thomas, which were growing ever nearer. "There's no time for this, Cora, we must go now," he said urgently.

"Oh, but it's just getting interesting," said Mrs Blake with a smirk. "Look at her little face trying to work it all out. Would you like me to tell you who you are, little girl? You really are clueless. You are..."

Sonny grabbed Alice's hands and turned her to face him. He seemed to be squeezing all his strength and warmth into her. "You're my sister," he said urgently, stealing the words from Cora Blake's lips. His words burst violently into the air, as the stars glittered above, the ocean ebbed and flowed and the Blakes stood silently watching.

"But...no," said Alice, limply. "That *can't* be true."

Sonny squeezed her hands again. "We have the same mother and father. I just didn't know it until today."

Alice's head pulsed. *Sonny was her brother.*

Cora Blake's laugh was bitter. "Your grandfather despised your father and his ambition to win the Blue Riband race. He promised us a fortune if we could stop him. Diamond Shipping were desperate for the *Sapphire* to keep the trophy and we were more than happy to help. It's quite ironic that the two of you – your grandfather's own flesh and blood – thwarted his plan."

Alice understood then that the Blakes' plan went

beyond the rivalry of two shipping companies vying for a coveted trophy. This was personal. But why had her grandfather taken such a strong dislike to her father? And how did Sonny fit in to what she knew of her family? She thought again of the envelopes of money in the trunk and shook her head, hoping for clarity.

"That's enough, Cora. As usual you've said far too much," said Mr Blake through gritted teeth. Striding over to Sonny he yanked his arm and dragged him away from Alice and round the deck equipment to the railing. "The children will have to come with us. It's the only way to silence them."

Fear reached out to Alice like a grey hand, touching her on the back of the neck. "No!" she screamed.

Sonny flailed around valiantly, but Mr Blake's rubber suit was slippery, and he could not get a firm enough purchase to wriggle free. Sonny threw a desperate look at Alice. He seemed to be saying a silent goodbye and steeling himself for what was about to happen next.

Chapter 33

OVERBOARD

Mr Blake stood by the railing, gripping Sonny's arm. There was nothing beyond them except the churning, pewter depths of the North Atlantic. If he took Sonny overboard with him, the boy would not survive.

"Let him go!" Alice demanded. She felt like a weathervane in a storm, her breaths coming fast and hard.

"What are you doing? This wasn't part of the plan," said Cora Blake, looking at her husband in surprise.

"These children have uncovered everything," Mr Blake said through gritted teeth. "You never did know when to stop talking."

Alice pressed her back into the metal drum she was standing against, terror gripping her throat.

Mrs Blake's face was granite hard. "It's as much your fault as mine. Nothing has gone right."

"You won't get away with this," said Sonny bravely, still struggling in Mr Blake's grip. He locked eyes with Alice again and she felt an unfamiliar sensation, as if they were now joined by a strong and unbreakable rope. *Her brother.*

Alice looked back up the steps, hoping to hear that help was on its way, but still the only sounds were the shudder of the ship steaming onwards, and the pulse of the ocean.

Cora Blake's lifebelt strap had come loose. She clicked her tongue in irritation and dipped her head to tie it. As she did, a small plastic wallet fell from where it had been wedged between her diving suit and her lifebelt and landed on the deck.

Alice took a deep breath as she stared at it. The fact the Blakes were taking it with them must mean it was important. She thought of Pearl on the *Titanic* and her brave and calm nature. She had not given up, even when all seemed to be lost. She thought of Sonny throwing the camera at Mr Blake when he had pulled out his gun. His courageous action had saved them all. Miriam had left her home behind and was brave and strong despite the troubles she had faced. Charlie had taken many risks to help them, his presence solid and unwavering.

Cora noticed the fallen wallet, gasped and dived for it.

Summoning all her courage, Alice darted forward, picked up the wallet first and ran back to the drum.

Cora Blake's head snapped up. "Give that back," she snarled.

"What's happening over there?" asked Mr Blake, grunting in his efforts to restrain Sonny, who was still wriggling valiantly.

"She's got our passports...and the camera film," said Cora, slowly approaching Alice.

Alice grasped the wallet tighter, realizing she held important evidence. This must be the film of photographs she had snapped in the engine room.

Mr Blake flashed a look at his wife. "You fool. I told you to drop the camera and film overboard."

Cora Blake's jaw tightened, and Alice sensed for the first time that she was uneasy. "I thought we may still get paid something by Diamond Shipping if we could prove we tried."

"Watch out, Alice!" called Sonny as Mrs Blake lunged forward, grasping for Alice and the wallet. But the bulky weight of her half-tied lifebelt made her stumble to her knees.

Stuffing the wallet into the pocket of her slacks, Alice quickly skirted around Mrs Blake and ran to the railings where Mr Blake held Sonny. She had an idea. It was perilous, but there was a small chance she could pull it off. "You might have hurt Joseph, but I won't let you do the same to my brother," she said to Mr Blake fiercely.

Mr Blake's eyes narrowed. "You've no idea what happened to Joseph."

"I was there," said Alice. "I heard your argument. I heard you push him." She threw an anxious glance at Cora Blake, who, with the combination of the rubbery diving suit and lifebelt, was struggling to get to her feet.

Mr Blake's eyes darkened. "The noise I heard up on the swimming pool balcony that day. It was you. You were spying on us even then. You little…"

"Don't, Alice. Don't say any more," begged Sonny, whose eyes were brimming with terror.

Alice took a deep breath. "I have the camera film and your passports. I'll tell the police what you've done, and I've the evidence to prove it," she said, patting her pocket and rooting her feet on the deck. "You've made mistake, after mistake, after mistake, after…"

Mr Blake reacted in just the way Alice hoped he would. His eyes incandescent with rage, he released Sonny and reached for Alice, but she had anticipated this and darted quickly to one side. The weight of Mr Blake's lifebelt made him tip forward like a domino.

"Over here," Alice called to Sonny.

Sonny ran to Alice, grabbed her hand, and pulled her away to the steps. "Well done," he said breathlessly, throwing her an impressed grin.

There was a commotion on the deck above and the clatter of feet. Four officers ran down the steps, one of them her father.

"What in heaven's name is happening here?" he said in disbelief, as two of the officers apprehended Mr Blake and hauled him to his feet. "Are you hurt?" he asked Alice and Sonny quickly.

"No," said Alice, as Sonny shook his head. "You need to stop her from getting away!"

The officers had captured Mr Blake, but Cora Blake was not ready to give up. Clambering to her feet, and throwing Alice and Sonny a withering look, she yanked her lifebelt straps tight and ran to the railings.

"Now then...don't do anything foolish," called Alice's father in horror, advancing slowly as the fourth officer rushed to assist.

Alice's heart pulsed in her throat.

With one last smirk, Cora Blake slipped over the side of the ship and disappeared.

Alice closed her eyes and winced, waiting for a distant splash.

"No...Cora!" cried Mr Blake with a sob.

"She'll be sucked under by the ship's propellors," Alice heard an officer say.

The wind stung Alice's cheeks and she held her breath.

"Look, Alice," said Sonny a moment later.

Alice opened her eyes to see Cora Blake being dragged back up over the rail by the straps of her lifebelt; her father and an officer were holding on tight.

"Good job you didn't do up the straps properly. They caught on the railings," the officer muttered.

Alice's legs buckled in relief.

"We did it. We stopped them," said Sonny, as the officers busied themselves with the Blakes, who were muttering furiously to one another.

"Father, you should have this," called Alice, pulling the wallet from her pocket. "There's a camera film of pictures we took in the engine room of the Blakes and Richardson conspiring to slow the ship. Mr Lewis, the chief engineer, was in on it too."

"Mr Blake is also responsible for hurting Joseph Wilks," chimed in Sonny. "He tried to kill him when Joseph refused to help with their plan."

"I've written everything down in my adventures scrapbook. You should look at that too," urged Alice.

Her father looked quite bewildered as he took the wallet and slipped it into his jacket pocket. "What on earth have you been up to? I thought you were occupied with your embroidery and library books, Alice."

Alice gave him a shrug, wondering how she would ever explain it all.

"I heard Joseph Wilks is waking up, Staff Captain. I'll send someone down to have a word with him," said one of the officers as he restrained Mr Blake.

Alice exchanged a delighted look with Sonny at this welcome news.

"That steward got what he deserved," snarled Mr Blake unpleasantly.

Father ignored Mr Blake and turned back to the officers. "Lock these people up in the isolation ward. Richardson and Mr Lewis are to be taken there too. I'm very disappointed in their bad characters and lack of loyalty to the *Queen Mary*."

Alice felt a grim sense of satisfaction that the Blakes

would be locked up in the very place they had sent her earlier that day.

"We won't forget this," snarled Cora Blake, as she disappeared through the door alongside her husband. The sharp edge to her voice made Alice's toes curl uncomfortably, but there was no need to be afraid. They were finally safe.

Her thoughts were interrupted by Miriam and Charlie clattering down the steps.

"Bravo," said Charlie with a grin, patting Sonny on the back.

"Hurrah," said Miriam, flinging her arms round Alice. "Good and brave people win in the end."

Alice smiled weakly. "Well done on raising the alarm. We did this together. All of us."

Pearl stood behind them in her dressing gown, her hair in curlers and a scarf. "Goodness, Alice. When you said a mystery needed solving, I wasn't expecting this. If you'd told me, I might have been able to help."

Alice smiled. "Oh, but you most definitely did help," she said, thinking of the bravery she had summoned while thinking of Pearl, and the lemon sherbets that had helped Sonny when he was feeling unwell in the engine room.

"It's almost midnight," Pearl continued, looking at

Miriam. "I'll take you back to your family, and as for you, Charlie, you should get to bed. The head liftman will no doubt want a word with you in the morning."

"Uh-oh," said Charlie, his face dropping.

Pearl gave him a wry smile. "Be honest about what's happened, and you may be surprised."

Alice saw her father approaching. He was staring at Sonny in a most peculiar way now that the Blakes had been dealt with. "Hudson? Is...is it really you? The message given to me in the wheelhouse said you were here with Alice. But how can that be?" he said, rubbing the back of his neck.

A strange numbness crept over Alice's face as everything came flooding back. She felt total and utter confusion. Sonny was her brother. Why had her father kept this from her? How had they become separated?

Sonny took a step forward. Reaching into his pocket, he pulled out a piece of paper. "I found this in the trunk in the hold. I know the truth. I know you are my father, and that Alice is my sister." His voice was small, but also brave.

As Alice watched her father take the paper and read it, she suddenly remembered seeing Sonny push it into his pocket just before Rocket had disappeared in the hold. With everything that had happened she'd clean forgotten about it.

Father looked up. "You've been in the hold? You've looked in the trunk?"

"I found the keys to Mother's luggage and the detective bureau card," explained Alice, her teeth chattering. "You were hiding things from me. I wanted to know the truth." She stared at the piece of paper Sonny had given her father. "What does it say?"

Their father wiped a hand over his cheeks. "I'm sorry. It was never meant to be like this. I will tell you everything... I just need...a moment." His chin trembled and he looked at Sonny as if he wanted to fold him into an embrace but didn't quite dare. It made Alice feel quite breathless.

"I need to speak with Dorothy," said Sonny simply.

Father's eyes flared in sudden recognition. "Yes of course. I see who you are now. You're travelling with the woman who keeps questioning me. But you've been on this ship for months..." His voice trailed off and the worry lines between his eyebrows deepened.

Miriam and Charlie were standing in stunned silence at the most recent turn of events.

"Staff Captain, it's dark, cold and late and these children have had a terrible shock," said Pearl. "Why not continue this conversation inside and I'll fetch some warm drinks?"

"Yes. Yes of course," said Father. He looked at Alice and Sonny earnestly. "And I promise to tell you the truth now, every last bit of it."

Chapter 34

REUNITED

A short while later Alice and Sonny sat on their father's bunk wrapped in warm blankets, Rocket's cage resting between them. While their father had looked wide-eyed at the arrival of Sonny with Dorothy in her dressing gown and the small mouse, he did not question it.

Taking a sip from the mug of creamy hot chocolate Pearl had made, Alice read again the letter Sonny had found in the trunk in the hold.

Hope & Son's National Detective Bureau
5th Avenue,

New York

14th April 1936

Dear Mr Townsend,

Thank you for your recent communication. As I said at our last meeting, we are sorry to report that we still have no leads as to the whereabouts of your fourteen-year-old son, Hudson Townsend.

Following the passing of Hudson's grandfather, Elliott Carmichael, in March of this year, we have explored all avenues to try and locate the child but have no leads.

I realize you are keen to resolve your family's troubles and reunite Hudson with his sister, Alice, and I assure you we are doing all we can.

I shall inform you immediately of any progress and can assure you that your regular payments allow our finest detectives to travel worldwide as they continue to search for him.

Yours sincerely,

R.A. Hope, Esq.

Alice looked up at her father, who was pacing the cabin, and then to Dorothy, who was sitting white-faced at the desk, warming her hands on a cup of tea. "How did this happen? Why were Sonny and I separated?" Alice asked, feeling it vital to ask the biggest question first.

Father swallowed and rubbed his cheeks. "Your mother and I met and married when we were very young. I was low in the ranks of a shipping company and had no formal education. She was American and travelling with her wealthy father. Putting it plainly, your grandfather, Elliott Carmichael, didn't think I was good enough for your mother. He was a man of money and means. He did everything in his power to separate us."

"But that's dreadful," said Alice with a frown.

Sonny gave a silent nod of agreement, as he opened Rocket's cage and took him out. "You never told me your mother was American," he said, glancing at Alice.

"And I thought your grandfather was British," said Alice. They had both made assumptions which meant they had never for one second considered they could be related as they uncovered their family's secrets.

"Your mother and I eloped. We worked at sea, your mother taking a job as a seamstress. She had a real talent for that. We were never in one place for long, so your grandfather failed to find us. We were happy and liked it that way," said Father, staring at Sonny.

Sonny gave his father a shy look as Rocket scampered over his knees.

Father shook his head in disbelief as he looked at his son. "First we were blessed with you, Sonny, and then, Alice, you came along two years later," he continued. "The shipping company we worked for encouraged crew to bring their families on board. They said it made for a happier working environment and life was good for us all."

"But then it changed," said Alice, noticing the light fading from her father's eyes.

"Yes. Just after you were born, Alice, your grandfather discovered which ship we were on and sent a letter," Father said, watching Rocket as he ran up Sonny's arm. "He'd learned he had grandchildren and was keen to meet you both. I was worried, but your mother insisted he'd changed and wanted to make amends. Alice was poorly the day of the meeting, so stayed with me on board ship in New York. Your grandfather sent a car to pick up Rose and Hudson. That was the last I saw of them."

"Grandfather kidnapped us?" exclaimed Sonny, his eyes widening. Rocket paused and sniffed, as if sensing the momentous nature of the words being spoken.

Alice remembered then what she had learned from the baroness. It was Sonny she had seen getting into the car on the dockside all those years ago with their mother, not Alice.

Father frowned. "You could put it like that, although I was assured you were looked after very well." He gave a shallow sigh. "I was heartbroken. To lose my wife and son... well it was terrible."

"What happened next?" asked Alice, keen to learn more.

"When Rose and Hudson didn't return to the ship, I went after them. But I was threatened by your grandfather and paid to stay away," said her father, his face darkening.

"That explains the money in the trunk," said Alice, glancing at Sonny.

Father nodded. "Yes. Elliott said he would make all our lives impossible if I didn't do as he asked. He would ruin my career and take Alice too. I tried to correspond with Rose, but she never replied. I assumed she was unable to as she would never have willingly stayed out of contact with us. In the end I reluctantly sent on some of her and Hudson's belongings, but I kept Rose's luggage trunks. I couldn't bear to part with them. I suppose I still hoped she and Hudson might find a way to return and we could resume our lives at sea."

Alice felt a flicker of sadness, as she finally understood the full story behind her mother's luggage and belongings. She wished with all her heart that things could have been different and her grandfather a kinder man.

Her father swallowed, as if mentally preparing himself for the next part of the tale. "I discovered later that your mother had died that same year after suffering from a short spell of influenza. I was devastated and redoubled my efforts to bring Hudson home, but your grandfather continued to threaten me." He lowered his head. "He was too rich and powerful and there was nothing else to be done."

"I didn't see my grandfather often, but when I did, he was always kind to me," said Sonny, cupping Rocket in his palms.

"I believe your grandfather loved you and your mother very much, Hudson, but he was a complicated and jealous man and felt great bitterness towards me. He had a strong love of the ocean, though, like I do. I sometimes felt we could have been friends if we could have just set aside our differences," said Father sadly.

"So when you heard our grandfather had died this year, you began searching for Sonny again," said Alice, looking once more at the letter from the detective bureau.

Father nodded. "I knew that Elliott Carmichael could threaten me no longer. I also felt it safe to invite you on board with me, Alice, after Aunt Laura's accident. I know how you've always longed to go to sea, and I felt dreadful denying you that pleasure, but I had to keep you safe in case your grandfather found some underhand way to get at you too."

Alice gave him a sorrowful smile, pleased to have finally gained an insight into more of her father's past decisions.

"I'd never spent a penny of the money your grandfather gave me, but then I decided to put it to good use," Father continued. "I employed detectives to look for Hudson and would meet with them each time the ship docked in New York. I was convinced he was somewhere in America, but the search proved fruitless."

"So that's why you visited the hold each time the ship docked in New York," said Alice, other pieces of the puzzle falling into place. "You were taking money to pay the detective bureau and filing away any correspondence you received."

"How in heaven's name did you hear about me visiting the hold?" asked Father in surprise.

"Oh...um...well I've been talking to some of the crew," said Alice, not wanting Charlie to get into hot water for passing on that information.

Father scratched his chin. "I see. Well, the hold seemed the safest place to store the money and gave me easy access to it. There are regular cabin inspections, you see – even I must suffer that. To be found with the money and correspondence in my possession would have raised uncomfortable questions about my past – things I wanted to keep buried."

Sonny gave Dorothy a hard stare. "Did you know my father was on board this ship? Is that why we've been beetling backwards and forwards between New York and Southampton for all these months?"

A cloud of guilt crossed Dorothy's face and she looked down. "Yes," she whispered. Her teacup trembled as she placed it on the saucer. "I didn't learn the truth until some legal documents needed signing after your grandfather's death. I found out he'd lied about your parents losing their lives in a motor-car accident. He hadn't even told me their real names. I also found out your father was alive and well and working on the *Queen Mary*."

"You should have told me," said Sonny dully, as Rocket wriggled from his palms and scampered across the bunk to Alice.

"I've looked after you for many years and have grown

extremely fond of you, Sonny. The thought of handing you over like a parcel to someone I didn't know and saying goodbye was...well, it was unthinkable," said Dorothy, pulling a cotton handkerchief from her dressing-gown pocket and twisting it between her fingers.

Rocket ran round Alice, his little nose sniffing at new and unfamiliar smells. Something else dawned on her then, as she thought of the photographs in Sonny's cabin, and how close he and Dorothy seemed in them. How Sonny had said she had changed on the *Queen Mary* and their closeness had been slipping away. "I think perhaps Dorothy didn't want to lose you, Sonny. That's why she kept Father a secret from you."

"Is that true?" asked Sonny, his eyes glazed.

Dorothy nodded and pressed her lips together. "It is. I extended our stay on this ship and decided to find out more about your father. I had to be sure he was kind and trustworthy before revealing the truth. I've been...so distracted, so tired with it all. I thought of little else. But then I got cold feet and...well...I decided we should leave."

Father shook his head sadly. "And I thought I was the only one on board with secrets to keep."

"I hope in time you can both forgive me," said Dorothy, bowing her head.

Alice felt a burst of sympathy. Dorothy was wrong to hide the truth from Sonny and her father, but she had done it to protect someone she loved. While misguided, she could perhaps understand how it had happened.

"There were other secrets too, like the two silk gloves," said Sonny, still looking at Dorothy.

Dorothy's handkerchief stilled in her hands.

Passing Rocket to Sonny, Alice fetched the two gloves from her cabin. Her father's eyes widened at the sight of them as she quickly explained how she'd found one glove at home and the other in Sonny's cabin.

Dorothy's frown deepened. "I wondered where the glove had got to. It was missing from my keepsake box after this morning's break-in."

"A break-in...on board this ship?" said Alice's father in alarm.

"Don't worry. It was the Blakes. I got blamed for it and locked up, but I'll explain all of that later," said Alice with a wave of a hand.

Father tilted his head. "I can't say I'm happy to learn about your exploits, Alice, but we'll leave that conversation for another time."

"Alice really was very brave," said Sonny earnestly. "Please don't be too cross."

Alice grinned at Sonny.

Father raised his eyebrows, then giving them a lopsided smile, he turned his attention back to the gloves. "These were your mother's favourites," he said, running a finger over the embroidered roses. "She dropped one on the dockside the day she left. How did you come to have the other, Dorothy?"

Dorothy leaned forward. "I found the glove hidden in the back of a drawer when I was helping to clear out Elliott Carmichael's home. I knew then, from the initials in the glove, that it belonged to Sonny's mother. I took it, thinking I would give it to Sonny as a keepsake when he was older."

Alice saw her father's face crumple then. It was a shock to see this calm and controlled man look so distraught. She went to comfort him, her own throat thick with tears.

"I'm sorry, Alice," he murmured into her hair as they embraced. "It seemed safer, and kinder, to say nothing about your past. I persuaded Aunt Laura to keep this from you too, but she was most unhappy about it. I think she was right, and I have made a terrible mistake." He turned to Sonny. "I'm sorry, Hudson. I've thought about you every day. I would never have given up looking for you."

Sonny stepped forward hesitantly and held out a hand. Father released Alice and clasped Sonny's fingers tight.

In that moment Father's eyes shone, his worry lines smoothed away, and he looked content.

Alice smiled, noticing that Sonny's thick eyebrows were the mirror image of her father's. They also shared a love for following the rules, with her, Miriam and Charlie often coaxing Sonny into situations that under any ordinary circumstances he would probably have walked away from. She wondered what similarities she and Sonny shared. It was a new and exciting thought that made her fizz inside.

Sonny released his father's hand and took a few hesitant steps over to Dorothy. "I don't blame you. You were trying to protect me. But I'm glad I know the truth."

Dorothy took a deep, shuddering breath. Her eyes shone with love. "Your father is a good and kind man. I'm glad you have been reunited."

"I've often wondered what having a family would be like. But discovering this today…it's just so big," Sonny said, giving Father and Alice an uncertain look.

Alice understood how Sonny felt. They had been thrust into a new and unexpected world with no warning or preparation. Her future life at school and home was hazy, as if enveloped in the same mist the ship had steamed through a few days earlier. "Maybe all we can do is get to know each other and be friends. We're the same people we were yesterday. No matter what's happened, nothing can change that," she said quietly.

Sonny's frown turned into a small smile. "Friends. Yes. I like that idea."

Their conversation was interrupted by the ring of the telephone. Father strode over to it and picked it up. "Yes. Yes. Thank you," he said to the person on the end of the line. Placing the receiver down, he turned to look at them all. "I know we have much more to discuss, but would you accompany me out on deck? There's something I'd like you to see."

Alice stood beside Sonny on the curved deck in front of the officers' quarters, flanked by Father and Dorothy. She pulled the blanket tight round her shoulders as the beginnings of an indigo dawn illuminated the water.

"There, do you see it?" Father said, pointing.

Alice followed his finger and saw the Lightship *Ambrose* sitting low in the water, its red hull and lights winking a greeting as the *Queen Mary* steamed past.

"The end marker for the Blue Riband race," whispered Alice.

"Did the ship do it? Did it cross the Atlantic in a faster time than the *Sapphire*?" asked Sonny.

Their father's eyes glittered. "Yes, by the skin of her teeth she did. The *Queen Mary* has won the trophy." He turned to Alice and Sonny. "I must say, while I'm concerned about what you've been up to for the last few days, I'm jolly proud of you both. If it hadn't been for your investigations and quick thinking, the Blakes would have hampered our chances of setting a new record for this crossing."

Alice and Sonny exchanged delighted grins.

A new thought occurred to Alice. "Did you know our grandfather owned Diamond Shipping and the *Sapphire*?"

Father nodded. "Yes, I read about that in the newspapers. I must admit, it made me very determined that the *Queen Mary* should steal the trophy from the *Sapphire*, even after your grandfather's death. But I see now I've been so obsessed with the past I've forgotten to live in the present. That must change."

Alice slipped a hand into her father's, and he gave it a light squeeze. Sonny reached for Alice's other hand and then for Dorothy's. They stood in a row of four looking across the flat-as-marble water as the coastline of America grew closer. Alice felt a deep and satisfying warmth, despite the morning chill. They had successfully prevented the Blakes from slowing down the ship and in doing so had uncovered long-held secrets about their own family. It was a new day and while she had no idea what it would hold for them all, she was hopeful it was going to be a very promising one indeed.

Chapter 35

NEW BEGINNINGS

After a few snatched hours of sleep, Alice and Sonny waited on Sun Deck for Miriam. Squat tugs pushed and pulled the *Queen Mary* up the murky Hudson River and past the magnificent Statue of Liberty, as seagulls coasted above their heads.

In the light of day, Alice felt a little shy and unsure about the revelations of the night before and she nibbled on a thumbnail. To learn she had a brother felt both marvellous and frightening all at once.

"You know...you can look after Rocket sometimes.

That's if you'd like to," said Sonny, who was peering over the railing at the tugs.

Some of Alice's anxiety slipped away and she grinned. She moved a little closer until their elbows were touching. "I'd like that." But then she wondered how it would be possible for her to care for Rocket if Sonny and Dorothy were to disembark from the ship that day. The thought she might lose her brother before she'd had the chance to get to know him made a lump spring to her throat.

"Hello," called Miriam with a wave.

To Alice's surprise she saw Miriam had arrived with her parents. Mr and Mrs Brunn listened intently as the three children went over everything that had happened on the voyage.

Mr Brunn shook Alice's and Sonny's hands firmly. "Thank you for looking after our daughter. It has been a difficult time and to know she had friends helping her...it is wonderful."

"Well, it was her helping us a lot of the time," said Alice with a smile.

Mrs Brunn gave Miriam a proud look. "You were all brave," she said.

"We must continue to be brave," said Miriam simply, throwing a quick glance at the glinting windows of the approaching New York skyline, and the country she would now call home.

A short while later Alice, Sonny and Miriam arrived at the hospital ward to a sight that made Alice's heart soar. Joseph was propped up in bed with a large bandage covering his head.

Charlie grinned as he sat on the chair beside his friend. "He decided to wake up at last."

"I've been told everything you did to stop the Blakes. I've a lot to thank you for," said Joseph, wincing as he sat up a little.

Charlie gave him a stern look and helped him plump his pillows until he was comfortable.

"They were beastly. We couldn't let them get away with hurting you," said Alice firmly, sitting on the edge of the bed.

"How's the bump?" asked Sonny, patting his own head.

"Sore," grimaced Joseph. "I'm being taken ashore for an X-ray, but the doctor thinks I'll make a full recovery after some time at home with my mum and brothers."

Charlie grinned. "You'll be able to give Peter the model of the *Queen Mary* you made for his birthday."

"I am glad about that," said Sonny.

"Me too," said Alice, pleased that Joseph would spend time with his family and recover after his ordeal. But she was still curious to know about the events leading up to his injury. "Do you mind telling us what happened with the Blakes? We would like to know the whole story."

"The Blakes were friendly," began Joseph, picking at a loose thread on his sheet. "They tipped me well on their first three voyages. Then on their fourth, the one before this, they asked me to take a package to the Pig and Whistle and leave it behind the bar. That same day I overheard them speaking. They clearly didn't want the *Queen Mary* to win the Blue Riband race. They gave me the package but because of what I'd overheard, I opened it. Seeing the gold and the note to R made me realize they were up to no good. I did a bit of investigating and used a hairpin to open their suitcases."

"Gosh. That was good thinking. I suppose you found their gun then?" suggested Alice, remembering her fear at discovering that herself.

"Yes," said Joseph, wrinkling his nose. "I knew something very bad was afoot, so I hid the package in one of the swimming-pool changing cubicles until I could decide what to do. The Blakes kept asking what I'd done with it and things got difficult. They began threatening me and demanded I hand the package over."

"They are the foulest of people," said Charlie, throwing his friend a concerned glance.

Joseph swallowed. "After seeing the gun, I was too frightened to tell anyone what I'd discovered. I knew the Blakes would try and pin everything on me if I did. But when Sonny asked me what was wrong, I was getting desperate and decided to seek his advice. We arranged to meet at the pool, and I intended to show him the package, but Mr Blake must have followed me. We argued and the last thing I remember is him pushing me."

"The Blakes will pay for what they did," said Miriam angrily.

"My father found the gun in the chief engineer's safe and has passed it to the police. He also had a ship's photographer develop the pictures we took in the engine room. You can see the Blakes handing the package of gold to Richardson as a bribe to slow the ship," said Alice.

Joseph lay back on his pillows. "The police paid me a visit this morning. They said the Blakes are likely to face charges of attempted murder, as well as bringing a weapon on board and bribery. Richardson and his uncle will also face charges. Diamond Shipping will be investigated to see what part they played in all of this too."

"That should mean they're all locked up for a very long time," said Charlie with satisfaction.

"Good," said Miriam, wiping her hands together as if ridding herself of the Blakes once and for all.

Charlie's expression softened as he looked at Alice and Sonny. "You do have something to thank the Blakes for though. If you hadn't begun investigating them then you might not have discovered that the two of you were brother and sister," he said with a bright smile.

Miriam clapped her hands together. "Yes. You are together again. That is all that matters now."

Alice saw a smile creep onto Sonny's lips. Miriam was right, being together again was all that mattered. But when she thought of their future together it was like looking at a blank page in her adventures scrapbook. What would it hold for them both?

It was lunchtime and most of the *Queen Mary*'s passengers had disembarked at Pier Ninety, among the bustle of cars, luggage and porters. After one night in port, new passengers would embark for an eastbound voyage to Southampton the next day.

A flurry of reporters and photographers interviewed the captain and Alice and Sonny's father about winning the Blue Riband trophy. Alice and Sonny stood to one side, listening keenly as their father spoke of the ship's record-breaking four-day passage across the Atlantic. When one of the reporters asked if there had been any hitches along the way, he threw an amused glance at Alice and Sonny. "Nothing that couldn't be overcome," he said, giving them both a surreptitious wink.

Alice wondered if he was thinking about the adventures scrapbook she had shown him earlier; his eyes had widened as he saw her newspaper clippings of his voyages and read the notes she had jotted down as she tried to solve the mystery.

"That is a very fine record of events, Alice. I should think the police will want to have a look at this and hear your account of things too," her father had said.

Buoyed up with pride, Alice grinned, feeling at that moment she could have attempted to swim the Atlantic herself.

Later in the afternoon, as their father and Dorothy talked quietly next door, Sonny sat beside Alice on her bunk, while Rocket nibbled on sunflower seeds in his cage. "We're going ashore to buy Dorothy a new camera later.

She's quite proud hers was used to solve a crime, even if it did end up being thrown overboard by the Blakes. We're also going to a pet shop to get a bigger cage for Rocket to live in," Sonny said with a grin, watching his mouse.

Alice glanced at Sonny, as she flicked through the pages of her adventures scrapbook. "But what about you? Where will *you* live now?" she asked.

Sonny shrugged. "I really don't know."

There was a knock on the door and Father looked in. "Could you come in here, please? There are some things we would like to discuss."

Standing in Father's cabin, Alice and Sonny looked at him expectantly as he cleared his throat.

"Dorothy and I have been making enquiries with your grandfather's lawyers. It seems most of his fortune was lost in the Depression, and Diamond Shipping is being sold to pay his debts. There would have been no fortune for the Blakes even if they had achieved their plan to slow the *Queen Mary*," said their father.

"The Blakes didn't know *all* of Grandfather's secrets then," said Sonny with a grimace.

"Quite. But aside from the small fund Dorothy has for Sonny's care, and the money your grandfather gave me, the two of you do have some inheritance," said Father.

"Both of us?" Alice said in surprise.

Sonny stepped forward, his hands bunching into fists. "I want nothing to do with my grandfather after the lies he's told."

Dorothy placed an arm round Sonny's shoulders. "Listen to what your father has to say first."

"You've inherited a steam yacht. She's called *The Lady Rose*," said Father, his eyes suddenly misting over.

"The boat's named after Mother!" exclaimed Alice.

"It's one of the largest private yachts afloat and is currently chartered in the Adriatic – that's in the Mediterranean Sea," said Father.

"Your father has a suggestion. He's due some shore leave in August. Maybe we could all spend a little time on the yacht over the summer before we decide what happens next," said Dorothy. "How would you feel about that?"

Father turned to Sonny. "I know the yacht belonged to your grandfather, but it was built for your mother. She told me all about it. She spent time there as a girl when she was around your age. I've also discovered that some of her belongings are still on board."

Alice grinned. "Mother's things! I would like to see them *very* much." She glanced at Sonny to see if he agreed, but to her dismay he looked deep in thought, as if this was not a good plan at all.

Sonny chewed on his lower lip. "I was looking forward to spending some time ashore. Maybe living in a house with a garden and getting some more animals."

Alice held her breath, thinking he was going to refuse. Then she saw a slow smile grazing her brother's lips.

"But yes. I would like to spend the summer with you all – that's if Rocket can come too," he said.

Dorothy and Father exchanged a look.

"The mouse is really no trouble," said Dorothy with a shrug.

"Fine," said Father with a mock-sigh.

"There is one thing," said Alice. "I was wondering about the money in Mother's trunk. Could we perhaps give some to Miriam's family...either as a gift or a loan? They left everything behind in Germany and have nothing."

Father nodded. "That's a jolly good idea. I would like to think of that money being put to good use. I'm sure your mother would have approved too." He paused and looked at Dorothy, who now seemed quite jittery. "There is one last thing you should know," he said.

"What is it?" asked Alice.

"*The Lady Rose* is being chartered by King Edward VIII

for a summer cruise," blurted out Dorothy, unable to contain herself any longer.

"The King of England!" cried Sonny, his eyes widening.

"He has paid for exclusive use of the yacht, so we will have to muck in with the crew. But it should be quite an adventure, if you're still interested, that is," Father said hopefully.

Alice felt a growing excitement. Summer exploring her mother's yacht with her reunited family, and with the King of England on board too!

Sonny nudged Alice's arm. "I think you'd better buy a new adventures scrapbook," he whispered.

Alice grinned, thinking of the silver pen her father had given her and all the things she would be able to write about. Only this time, Sonny would be firmly by her side and, whatever the future held for them all, she was confident they would face it together.

My inspiration behind writing
PERIL ON THE ATLANTIC

When I was younger, my scientist dad would sometimes take sabbaticals abroad for work and we'd often travel to our destination by sea. One of my earliest memories is crossing the equator on a ship called the *Edinburgh Castle* when I was three years old, and I've also sailed across the Atlantic several times, inched slowly through the Panama Canal, travelled from Australia to the South Pacific Islands and more recently taken some multi-generational family trips by ship to Hawaii, around the Caribbean islands and the Mediterranean.

On our travels I've always been captivated by the sea's vastness, the huge empty skies, flat horizons and then the excitement of constantly arriving at new destinations and meeting such a range of people on board. On one transatlantic crossing I met some school children who were on board the ship for three months! They took lessons with their teachers in the morning and explored the ship and the ports we docked at in the afternoons. On another voyage we met a lady who had sold her home and lived permanently on board and was on first name terms with all the crew. I remember feeling a spike of envy at the time (what a way to live!) but I also wondered if this would be a little lonely. All these experiences helped inspire *Peril on the Atlantic* and some of the characters in the story.

Before I began to write this book, I had to decide what ship my characters would travel on. I remembered that some years ago while I was at university, my parents and brother had been in America and stayed on the *RMS Queen Mary*, a British ocean liner no longer in use. The ship is now berthed at Long Beach in Los Angeles and is a hotel and museum and my family had some great adventures exploring it.

I began to research the *Queen Mary* in more detail, and the more I read about this ship, the more I fell in love with her. She was launched by Cunard Line in 1936 and was billed as one of the fastest and most luxurious liners afloat, with her dining areas and lounges, swimming pools, a grand ballroom, a squash court and even a small hospital and dog kennels.

The ship set a new standard for transatlantic travel, with many viewing her as the only way to travel. Indeed, the ship was frequented by many celebrities of the time, including Fred Astaire, who makes a fictional appearance in my story (but really did tap-dance on the railings), Judy Garland and Clark Gable, and even Edward VII and Wallis Simpson and their dogs (and 120 pieces of luggage!). During the *Queen Mary*'s time at sea, she carried over two million passengers in peacetime and 810,000 military personnel in the Second World War, when she provided a vital role as a troop carrier.

The *Queen Mary* was also the recipient of the prestigious Blue Riband a number of times, the trophy awarded to the ship crossing the Atlantic in the fastest time – although as far as I know there were no sabotage attempts made on these voyages!

I hope you've enjoyed reading about my inspiration for Alice and Sonny's first mystery at sea. The great news is that the duo will return soon with a new mystery to solve, this time in the beautiful Mediterranean on a voyage with King Edward VII and Wallis Simpson, a poisonous octopus and priceless opal. What could possibly go wrong?

Turn the page for a sneak preview of Alice and Sonny's next adventure in

THE ROYAL JEWEL PLOT

"It's very different to the *Queen Mary*," said Sonny, looking around.

"The *Lady Rose* is smaller, but perfect," said Alice with a grin, peering over the side of the vessel. Mooring lines were being unhooked and the carpets on the quay rolled up as the crowds of people who had come to greet the king thinned out. They were preparing to depart.

"Goodness, this is quite something!" said Sonny.

Alice turned to see him standing beside Don in front of an ornate aquarium. It was as tall as she was and probably the width of her arms, if she stretched them out wide. The tank's four brass legs were fashioned into seahorses, with shells and fishes adorning the metal rim which supported the glass. On top of the lid stood a brass plate.

DANGER: DO NOT REMOVE LID

Stepping over to the boys, Alice peered into the tank. Layers of dark sand and grit were peppered with clusters of blue-grey rocks and stones. Silky green plant fronds waved gracefully like trees in a breeze. But while all of this was magnificent, it was a black iridescent stone the size of two thumbs sitting amidst it all that caught her attention.

"That's the black opal. It's very rare and was found in Australia," said Don, staring at it too. "It's so special it's impossible to put a value on it. It was on loan from an

American jewellery store to the previous owner of the yacht, Elliott Carmichael."

"Our grandfather," said Sonny, giving Alice a sidelong glance.

Alice pressed her lips together.

"But why did our grandfather want this opal on his yacht?" asked Sonny.

"My father said it was good business for the jewellery store and for the yacht as it attracted many wealthy people on board to see it, including the king," said Don. "But now the opal's been sold. When we arrive in Dubrovnik in four days, someone from the store is coming to collect it. They'll take it back to America to the new owner."

Alice scrunched her nose. "But why keep such a valuable gem in an aquarium and not locked away in a vault or a safe?"

"Look," said Sonny, pointing to a ripple of movement to the rear of the tank.

Alice swallowed a gasp, as a thin, brown, suckered arm reached out from a narrow crevice between two sizeable rocks. The arm lightly touched the opal, which was glittering blue, red and green in a spear of sunlight filtering through a gap in the awning above. The bulbous head of an an octopus, no larger than a golf ball, slithered out of the crevice, followed by its remaining arms. As Alice continued to watch, the octopus's arms began to change colour and were soon covered in faint blue rings. "What is happening?" she breathed.

"It's marvellous," breathed Sonny in delight. "Octopuses have special skin cells which means they can change colour to blend in with their surroundings."

Don glanced at the lid of the aquarium and the brass sign. "This is Olive, a rare blue ringed octopus from the Pacific Ocean, one of the deadliest species ever discovered. One bite from her means certain death. That's why the opal can be safely kept on display in the aquarium."

Alice stood away from the tank, goosebumps pricking her arms.

Sonny's jaw dropped. "Is it safe? To have a poisonous octopus on board I mean?"

Don shrugged. "The crew feed her through a hole in the top of the tank and wear thick gloves. My father says no one's been bitten so far."

A shiver danced across Alice's shoulders as she watched Olive alight upon a rock and curl her arms around it. "So Olive is guarding the opal."

"No one would ever risk stealing it while she's in there," agreed Don.

"You know a lot about sea creatures," said Sonny, throwing Don an impressed look.

"There's so much to see in the waters around here, sea horses, spider crabs, dolphins, and even turtles. I've a book on marine life I borrowed from the yacht's library. I'll show it to you if you like? I can even lend you a diving mask and we can go exploring," said Don with a smile.

"I'd like that very much," said Sonny. "What do you think, Alice?"

Alice chewed on a thumbnail and gave a noncommittal shrug. Sonny was a strong swimmer, but she wasn't. The thought of being in the water teeming with all this marine life sounded unnerving.

The yacht's whistle sounded, and the deck juddered under their feet. Turning once more to the railings, Alice saw the *Lady Rose* pushing away from the quay, the clear waters becoming murky as the propellors churned up sediment from the seabed.

The waving crowds were a blur of colour now, as the church bell on the hill tolled a final goodbye. They were off on a new adventure!

Find out what happens when Olive and the opal go missing in
MYSTERIES AT SEA: THE ROYAL JEWEL PLOT

Acknowledgements

In March 2021 I nervously sent my lovely agent Clare Wallace the idea for a historical series set at sea. Her reply was, "I LOVE IT". A huge thank you, Clare, for believing in the series from the very beginning and championing it all the way – I'm so lucky to have you by my side.

A big thank you to everyone at Usborne, with a special thanks to my fabulous editors Becky Walker and Alice Moloney for their excellent editorial chats and helpful notes – I love working with you both and I appreciate everything you do. Thanks also to Helen Greathead and Susanna Davidson for the inspired copyedits and sensitivity read.

Thank you to the Usborne marketing and publicity team, especially Fritha (when are we going for that coffee?), Hannah and Jess and all of your brilliant promotional ideas.

I had a vague hope for what the cover of this book might be like, and the amazing Will Steele and Marco Guadalupi exceeded this by a million – thank you, Will and Marco for your fabulous illustrations.

Thank you also to my friends and family, especially Jeremy, Jack, Ed and my mum who are endlessly supportive of me and my writing. My lovely dad took me on many ocean adventures when I was young, all of which helped inspire this series. The look of excitement on his face when I told him these books would be published was pure magic. This story is for him.

My final thanks go to all the writers, authors, booksellers, teachers, book bloggers and reviewers and readers who have been so supportive of my career. I couldn't do this job without you, so THANK YOU from the bottom of my heart.